**"You will pay, my girl,
for what your brother has done."**

Andreas's voice deepened, driving
the bitter words like nails into
Gemma's bewildered mind. "You will
pay in kind...in shame, and your
family's shame. You will stay here and
work in this house as my servant, as
Maria worked for your brother, and I
shall take you as and when I please,
as he took her."

Gemma swallowed. For a terrible
moment she'd had an image of those
firm lips crushing hers, those lean,
brown hands caressing her. She
whispered, "Touch me and I'll
kill you."

He laughed. "You have spirit. I
approve of that. Our time together
should prove more pleasurable
than I anticipated!"

Books by Sara Craven

HARLEQUIN PRESENTS

HARLEQUIN ROMANCE

These books may be available at your local bookseller.

Don't miss any of our special offers. Write to us at the following address for information on our newest releases.

Harlequin Reader Service
P.O. Box 52040, Phoenix, AZ   85072-2040
Canadian address: P.O. Box 2800, Postal Station A,
5170 Yonge St., Willowdale, Ont. M2N 6J3

SARA CRAVEN

alien vengeance

Harlequin Books

TORONTO • NEW YORK • LONDON
AMSTERDAM • PARIS • SYDNEY • HAMBURG
STOCKHOLM • ATHENS • TOKYO • MILAN

CHAPTER ONE

'You say there's still no message for me?' Gemma Barton looked her incredulity at the desk clerk. 'Are you sure?'

'Quite sure, *thespinis*.' The man spread his hands apologetically and smiled at her, his teeth very white under the heavy Cretan moustache. 'It is important this message? It worries you that it has not come?'

Gemma gave a slight shrug. 'Actually, I'm more disappointed than worried,' she returned. 'But I'll get over it. The only problem is I don't quite know what my plans are until I do hear from my brother, and tonight is the last night of my booking here.'

'No problem,' came the instant assurance. 'It is early in the season still, and there is room if you wish to stay. You have only to let us know.'

Well, that was reassuring at any rate, Gemma thought as she walked across the foyer and through the archway into the breakfast room. Not that she was sure she wanted to stay on in Heraklion even though the hotel was cheap and friendly and spotlessly clean. As she had another ten days to spend on Crete, she might as well make the most of them and travel further afield—especially if Mike continued to be conspicuous by his absence.

He was and always had been the limit, she reminded herself ruefully as she helped herself to fresh bread rolls, and poured orange juice into her glass. Mike was mad on botany, and generally oblivious to anything else, and the world's worst correspondent, causing their mother, Gemma knew, hours of silent worry when he vanished into the wide blue yonder on his everlasting field trips.

This prolonged visit to Crete was part of a postgraduate study he was doing, and it had been his own idea that Gemma should join him for a holiday, instead of making one of a party to Ibiza with some of the women she worked with.

'This is the place,' one of his scrawled missives had told her. 'Away from the tourist bits, the living is dirt cheap, and I've fallen on my feet, residing in the lap of luxury half way up a mountain. You could do the touristy things for a couple of days, then come and see the real Crete with me.'

'The real Crete,' their mother had snorted. 'That mountain he mentions is probably all his dirty laundry.'

Gemma was inclined to agree, but at the same time the idea of going to Crete had taken a definite hold on her. While she was still at school she'd read Mary Renault's *The King Must Die* and the exploits of Theseus and his fellow bull dancers at the Minoan court had fired her imagination.

And she wasn't going to pass up the chance of going there, even if it did mean dealing with a backlog of Mike's dirty shirts and socks.

So, she'd fixed her flight, and written to tell him, not being amazed or aghast when she received no reply except a postcard of the harbour at Chania with a laconic 'Great' and his initial scribbled on it.

It was rather a blow, however, to arrive at Heraklion airport and find he wasn't there to meet her, but she supposed she could have expected it with Mike's track record, and was glad she'd taken the trouble to book herself a few nights' bed and breakfast at a hotel not too far from the harbour.

That very first day, even before she had unpacked, she'd written again to Mike—briefly reminding him that she'd arrived, and giving the name and address of the hotel and its telephone number. Each day since she'd expected to hear from him, but there'd been no word at all. Gemma wasn't a child any more. She didn't need a big brother to hold her hand, particularly on Crete where the people, she was sure, must be among the friendliest and most hospitable in the world. She knew Mike was there to work, and if he was too busy to get away, and regretting his rash suggestion then all he had to do was say so.

There was plenty she could do. She'd made friends with a young couple, fellow-guests at the Hotel Ariadne already, and they were talking about hiring a car and taking a leisurely trip right round the island, staying at tavernas en route. If Gemma cared to share the petrol costs, she was welcome to go with them, and she was sorely tempted.

But—she did want to see Mike, or at least talk to him so that she could take reassuring news home to her mother, who was still rather low after a lingering virus infection she'd acquired in the early spring.

As she turned away from the buffet with her food, she saw James and Hilary waving madly at her from a table in the corner of the room, and went over to join them.

'Ignore James,' was Hilary's greeting as she sat down. 'He was introduced to *raki* last night and the friendship developed rather too quickly, so he's feeling a little fragile today. Says he can't face the bus ride to Knossos. But I'm still going,' she added swiftly, seeing faint disappointment on Gemma's face. 'I hope you are too.'

'I wouldn't miss it,' Gemma said, giving the wan James a sympathetic grin. 'Firewater was it?'

James groaned. 'I only noticed the fire. Hilly, of course, stuck virtuously to *ouzo* and is fine. There's no justice.'

His wife wrinkled her nose at him and turned to Gemma. 'Takis says the bus to Knossos leaves regularly from the harbour.'

'Then Takis is a liar,' James said, taking a cautious sip of coffee. 'He knows as well as we do that Cretan buses run as and when they feel like it. I don't know why they even bother to have a timetable.'

'Hangovers don't suit James. They make him so jaundiced,' Hilary said regretfully. 'The first couple of days we were here, he thought it was wonderful that nothing ever happened when it was supposed to. Said it was the first real holiday he'd ever had.'

'I still say that,' James maintained. 'And Takis doesn't believe in buses anyway. He told me so. He says you should be able to walk the five kilometres or so to Knossos like they used to do in the old days—two big strong girls like you.'

'Carrying bundles of firewood on our heads, no doubt,' Gemma said drily. 'There are times when Takis asks for a punch in the throat.'

'Well, don't expect Penelope to give him one,' Hilary advised cheerfully. 'She thinks the sun, moon and stars shine out of him, and she'd probably walk to Knossos and back carrying him on her head if he asked her to.'

'Cretan men have got it made,' James said moodily. 'They don't allow any women's liberation nonsense to interfere with their basic rights.'

Hilary giggled. 'And nor do you, darling, nor do you. In fact, you and Takis have a lot in common, and you can spend a lovely day together drinking coffee under the awning and discovering what it is while Gemma and I acquire some culture.' She looked at her watch. 'We'll meet in the foyer in twenty minutes shall we? Then, with any luck, we'll get to the Palace before it's too hot.'

'It's too hot already,' said James.

He had a point, Gemma thought as she and Hilary threaded their way along the busy streets leading to the harbour a little while later. Only idiot tourists rushed round risking sunstroke. Her skin was already beginning to tan, in spite of the filter creams she used to protect it, and on her first day in Heraklion she'd invested in a cheap straw hat.

The tables in the shade of the pavement cafes were already doing a roaring trade, she saw, and the aroma of coffee and cooking food mingled with the all pervasive fumes from the traffic. All around them worry beads clicked in an eternal rhythm, and voices hummed and rose on notes of laughter or expostulation. There never seemed to be any muttered conversations, Gemma thought with amusement. If a Greek wanted you to know something, he let you have it full blast.

They were equally uninhibited in other ways too, she reminded herself, aware of the frankly appreciative dark-eyed glances pursuing Hilary and herself as they walked along. At home she would have found such openly expressed admiration both embarrassing and a nuisance. Here, it was distinctly heartwarming to be regarded as if you were Aphrodite rising from the waves.

To their surprise, the Knossos bus was already there and filling up when they arrived. They found seats without difficulty, and paid the few drachmas for the fare.

They were both quiet as they set off, Hilary checking the cartridge in her camera, and Gemma wondering what it must have been like to have been part of the Athenian tribute to King Minos, and to have started the weary trudge in the sun to Knossos knowing that danger and probable death awaited them there.

She was very glad, she thought, that she lived in the 1980s instead of a couple of thousand years B.C. and that no danger waited for her at Knossos, or anywhere else on Crete.

Even as the thought formulated in her mind, a slight shiver went through her, as if a hand had been laid on her shoulder and a warning voice breathed in her ear, 'Be careful. No Greek would ever tempt the fates and you shouldn't either.'

It was an odd, disturbing little moment, as if a sudden shadow had passed across the sun, then Hilary made some idle remark about the suburbs they were passing through, and it was gone.

As journeys went it was relatively dull, the bus passing through the usual urban sprawl. Hilary mentioned the projected trip to the White Mountains and asked if Gemma had given it any further thought.

'I'd love to come,' Gemma admitted. 'And I can't wait forever for Mike to get in touch. After all, I don't even know if he got my last message. Perhaps this mountain retreat of his has no telephone, or the mail only gets delivered once a month.' She sighed. 'Or more probably, Mike's gone prancing off up some crag after a rare herb, and hasn't given me another thought.'

Hilary sent her an amused look. 'Does he do things like that?'

Gemma nodded. 'Constantly.'

Hilary chuckled. 'Then I suggest you set him a deadline, say midnight tonight. If he's not in touch by then, you come with us. How about that?'

'It sounds good to me,' Gemma agreed. She glanced round, aware of an unusual stir. 'What's everyone looking at? We're not there yet are we?'

'The most amazing car is following us,' Hilary said. 'They're all lost in admiration, I suppose.' She grimaced slightly. 'Thank God James isn't here, or he'd be off the bus by now and interrogating the driver about cylinders and camshafts and all the other things he finds so fascinating.' She eyed Gemma narrowly. 'Do they fascinate you too, or do you consider a car to be an unreliable lump of tin, designed to get one from A to B, like me?'

Gemma grinned. 'I think I occupy the middle ground. But I must admit it is a beautiful car—Italian, I think. It must have cost a fortune.

Hilary shrugged. 'Well, the gentleman behind the wheel looks as if he can well afford it,' she commented casually. 'You admire the car, and I'll admire him.'

The car, Gemma thought, was worth a second or even a third look. Not even the inevitable coating of Cretan dust could detract from its sleek, powerful lines. The top was down, so she was afforded a full view of the driver, but she was not particularly impressed, she told herself.

He was undoubtedly Greek, black haired and olive-skinned. His eyes were masked by sun glasses, but they did not disguise the fact that he was classically, almost startlingly good-looking.

In fact, Gemma allowed judiciously, he would almost have been beautiful, but for the tough uncompromising lines of his mouth and chin.

She thought that he must be aware of the fact that he was under close scrutiny from the bus, but preferred to appear arrogantly unaware of the fact.

'Pseud,' she thought dismissively, but watched with unwilling approval as he, at last, overtook the bus with maximum leeway, but minimum effort. He wasn't her type, but he knew his car and how to handle it.

'I expect he's one of those Greek tycoons one reads about,' Hilary said dreamily. 'Maybe we'll meet him, stumbling round the ruins at Knossos. If he's smitten, and invites you to cruise on his yacht, I hope you won't feel bound by our prior invitation.'

'He's more likely to be someone's chauffeur, joy-riding on his day off,' Gemma said crushingly. 'And if he does have a yacht, it will probably be already crammed to the gunwales with starlets.'

Hilary sighed extravagantly, 'Oh, Gemma, you're so prosaic sometimes. Don't you like to fantasise a little?'

Gemma smiled. 'Why, yes, but my fantasies don't centre round macho Greeks driving cars like virility symbols.'

Hilary gave her a curious look. 'Just for the record—is there anyone serious?'

Gemma shook her head rather wryly. 'No one,' she admitted. 'They used to say that it was women who wanted to get serious, who always had marriage in mind, but it seems to me that every man I meet wants to rush me into—into some kind of commitment or other, and I'm just not ready for that. Perhaps it's a fault in me but I like to take my relationships slowly—one step at a time, but they seem to want—instant *rapport*.'

Hilary smiled drily, 'You're right to be cautious.

I used to be that way myself, then I met James and within a month we were engaged. Don't freeze them all off, Gemma, or you could miss out on something wonderful.'

Gemma laughed. 'Not so far, I haven't, and that I can guarantee, I'm afraid.' She leaned forward. 'It looks as if we're nearly there.'

On leaving the bus, they walked down the narrow road towards the Palace, skirting the tavernas and souvenir shops, threading their way gingerly between the cars parked at the side of the road.

There was traffic edging down the road all the time, and in spite of herself, Gemma found she was watching out for an opulent dark blue sports car.

'I'm letting Hilary's nonsense get to me,' she told herself severely.

'It's too hot for much culture,' Hilary said as they queued up at the admission gate behind a party of French, who'd arrived with their own guide and were arguing noisily about numbers. 'I vote we belt round, then go and find something cold to drink.'

But inside the gate, it was like stepping into a different world. There were trees and shade, and Gemma saw that people were moving more slowly, talking more quietly, as if in respect of the fact they were present in one of the ancient places of the earth.

Even Hilary seemed subdued as they walked up the causeway towards the Palace ruins. It was all so much vaster than Gemma had imagined and not even the amount of restoration work which had been carried out, and the crowds of people wandering about could affect the power of its atmosphere.

By mutual consent, they decided not to attach themselves to any of the official tours which were being conducted round. Instead they walked quietly through the remnants of corridors and courtyards, past the remains of sacrificial altars, trying to come to terms with the size of the place.

They looked at restored frescoes, glowing in the brilliant sun, and wandered through dark state chambers where once King Minos and his Queen had sat in splendour.

Hilary was busy with her camera, making Gemma pose for her against painted columns, beside the big pottery jars, tall enough to conceal a man, and near the great Bull's horns carved in stone, a chilling reminder of the Minotaur myth.

It was while they were standing studying the fresco of the Lily-Prince that Gemma first felt they were being watched. She told herself she was being silly. There were dozens of other people around, all doing the same thing as themselves. It was the young Priest-King with his plumes and flowing locks which was the real centre of attention, as a casual glance around confirmed.

All the same she was glad to be back in the open air again.

Hilary looked around at the clustering hills and tall cypresses which bordered the enclosure fence like sentinels. 'It can't have been too easy to defend—in a valley like this,' she remarked dubiously.

'They wouldn't have had to,' Gemma said. 'It wasn't a fortress. It was a symbol of how powerful and mighty the Cretan empire was. People came here to pay their respects, not attack.'

Hilary grinned. 'They probably came to admire the drainage,' she said. 'It says in my book that the Queen's apartments had the first recorded flush loo. I like that—a homely touch among all this fallen splendour. And talking of splendour, just look at that.'

In a corner, rooted among fallen stones and rubble, a huge bush was just beginning to break into delicate blue blossom.

Hilary pushed Gemma gently. 'Go and stand by it, love. I want one last photograph.'

Gemma obeyed, waiting while Hilary adjusted the camera, muttering to herself, and motioned to her to alter her position fractionally.

'Remember, don't smile,' Hilary cautioned. 'Just look up when I say your name.'

Gemma stared down at the dusty ground. She heard Hilary call out, 'Gemma' and glanced up, trying to look into the sunlight without blinking, and saw a figure standing behind Hilary, tall and dark in the brilliance. She knew him at once. It was the driver of the car which had followed the bus—Hilary's supposed tycoon. He was the last person she had ever expected to see again. But even as she registered all this, her shocked mind told her something else—that he was terrifyingly, blazingly angry. She felt her face go rigid, as if she was bracing herself against some blow, and heard Hilary groan.

'I may have said "don't smile", but there's no need to look as if you'd just seen Marley's ghost. Wait one second while I take another.'

Gemma closed her eyes, passing the tip of her tongue over her dry lips. When Hilary spoke again, and she looked up, the man had gone.

She thought feebly, 'It's the sun. I'm seeing things.'

But she knew she wasn't. On the face of it, he was an unlikely sightseer, but he'd been there.

And anyway, she adjured herself impatiently, it

was wrong to judge by appearances. Perhaps he wasn't a chauffeur or a wealthy playboy, but an expert on the Minoan period.

His unexpected appearance could be rationally explained, but she couldn't justify to herself that odd sense of his rage she'd experienced as he looked at her.

She hadn't simply been surprised to see him. She'd felt threatened—frightened even. And yet there was no logical reason for it. They were strangers to each other—she knew they were.

She thought, 'If I'd ever met him, I'd remember. And now that I've seen him again, I have a feeling I won't forget him in a hurry.'

Hilary joined her, putting her camera back into its case. She said, 'Are you all right. You look a bit green round the gills. Is it the sun?'

Gemma forced a smile. 'Maybe. What about that cold drink you mentioned?'

All the way back to the gate, she had to resist an impulse to look over her shoulder and see if he was following. She told herself that she was being a complete idiot. She was imagining things, that was all. The sun, the power of the ruins, her worry over Mike had all conspired against her suddenly, and knocked her off balance. A cold beer, she thought, and something to eat would restore her normal equilibrium.

They bought some postcards and walked slowly back up the hill, turning thankfully into the vine-covered shade of one of the tavernas. The waiter was playing water from a hosepipe on to the floor, and the air smelled fresh and cool as they sat down.

They ordered beer and souvlaki—little chunks of lamb grilled on skewers and served with french fried potatoes, and a Greek salad of cucumbers, tomatoes, peppers and fetta cheese, dressed with herbs and olive oil. Gemma sat and looked through the guide book, while Hilary wrote a couple of postcards and changed the cartridge in her camera.

Other people started to come in. Some Germans took the next table, and one of them had a radio playing music softly. The beers, when they arrived, were ice cold and Gemma began to feel relaxed.

Then Hilary said under her breath, 'Hell's bells. You're never going to believe who's just walked in.'

Gemma put down her glass. She said too brightly, 'Not the mystery tycoon?'

'As ever was.' Hilary's tone sharpened. 'My God, he's looking right at us. Supposing he comes over . . .'

Gemma remembered the force of the curious anger. She said, 'He won't come over.'

'No, you're right,' Hilary conceded. 'He's taken one of the far tables, but he's facing this way, and it's you he's looking at.' She grinned. 'Maybe that cruise is on, after all.'

Gemma's mouth was dry, and she took another sip of beer. 'I really don't think so.'

The food was on its way, but she wasn't hungry any more. She was remembering how she'd felt she was being watched near the corridor of Processions—how he'd appeared out of the blue when Hilary was photographing her, and now here he was again—as if he was following them.

If she could look at it from Hilary's light-hearted viewpoint, it would almost be flattering, but somehow that wasn't possible.

She pushed her food around, going through the motions of eating, but her appetite had died on her completely.

This, she told herself stormily, is really ridiculous—allowing a total stranger to put me off a meal I'm going to have to pay for anyway.

With a feeling almost of defiance, she ate the last few morsels of lamb, and mopped up the salad juices with a piece of crusty bread, before asking the attentive waiter to bring her some ice cream.

As she did so, she looked towards the stranger for the first time, and realised with a tremor of apprehension that he was watching her. He'd removed his dark glasses, and without their concealment, she had to admit he was stunningly attractive, his swarthy face brooding and enigmatic.

Their glances met—locked, and Gemma felt her cheeks redden as his firm lips twisted in a contemptuous little smile, and the dark eyes looked her over in an insolent, overtly sexual appraisal.

Mortified, Gemma tore her gaze away. She thought savagely, 'If I went near any yacht of his, I'd sink it.'

Hilary said in an undertone, 'He can't take his eyes off you, Gemma.'

'Don't I know it.' Gemma pushed away the remains of her melting ice cream. 'Do you think we could have the bill, and get out of here?'

But this wasn't as easy as it sounded. The waiter was clearly upset by their intended departure. He offered them coffee, he offered them more beers, he offered cigarettes from his own pack, produced with a flourish from his shirt pocket. Gemma smiled tautly and refused, and asked for the bill, all the time tormented by the burning conviction that the stranger was deriving sardonic amusement from this little piece of by-play.

As they left, amid the waiter's lamentations,

Gemma found herself praying that they wouldn't be followed.

She could hardly believe the state she was in. She thought impatiently, 'Oh, get a grip on yourself. There's nothing sinister in all this. We're two girls on our own, and he's the predatory type. He probably thinks he's God's gift to the female sex, and that his technique is infallible.'

To do him justice, with his looks, she doubted whether he would have many failures.

But all the same, she felt on edge all the time they were waiting for the bus to come.

Hilary said teasingly, 'Your problem, Gem, is that you don't know when you're on to a good thing.'

Gemma shook her head. 'He is not a good thing,' she said. 'Believe me.'

The bus came at last, and as she climbed aboard, Gemma took a last jittery look over her shoulder. The stranger, however, was nowhere to be seen, either on foot or in his car.

She felt an overwhelming sense of relief. Soon, she'd be back in the safe anonymity of Heraklion, and tomorrow she'd be driving towards Chania with James and Hilary on the next stage of her holiday, and she'd be able to put this oddly annoying series of incidents out of her mind.

But as she went into the hotel, Takis the manager hailed her from behind the reception desk. 'Ah, Kyria Barton. There is a message for you.' He turned to the pigeon holes behind him and extracted an envelope. It bore the single typed word 'Gemma'.

She thought, 'Mike—at last.'

She smiled at Takis. 'When did this arrive?'

'Just after you and Kyria Trent had left for Knossos. Spiro says there was first a phone call, and he explained you had gone out. Then when he came back from coffee, this letter had been left for you.' Takis nodded paternally. 'This pleases you, *ne*?'

Gemma tore open the envelope and scanned the single typewritten sheet within.

'Dear Gemma,' it said. 'Something has come up which prevents my meeting with you in Heraklion as you suggest. Perhaps instead you could come here to the Villa Ione in Loussenas. There is only one bus a week, so I suggest you hire a car and a driver. Make no attempt to drive yourself, as the road is very bad in places. Michael.'

'Is it good news, or bad news?' Hilary asked.

Gemma shook her head. 'I'm honestly not sure. He wants me to join him, but he sounds very curt about it.' She sighed. 'Perhaps I'm being a nuisance. Maybe I'll drop him another line, telling him to forget it and make the trip to Chania after all.'

She handed the note to Hilary, who read it through in silence. Then she said, 'You don't think he's sick or in trouble of some kind?'

Gemma groaned. 'That's just what I was wondering. Knowing Mike, it could be both, but he wouldn't want to spoil my holiday by involving me.' She bit her lip. 'I'm going to have to hire this car as he says and go to him.'

'You'll do nothing of the kind,' Hilary contradicted. 'We'll drive you to this Loussenas, wherever it is. If it's in the mountains it should be spectacular, and we're in no great hurry to get to Chania in one day.'

'I can't ask you to do that,' Gemma protested.

'You haven't asked,' Hilary said firmly. 'I'm telling you what's going to happen. And James will say exactly the same, so no arguments.' She gave Gemma back her note, and added a comforting pat on the shoulder. 'And now I'm going up to have a shower. Takis, I hope the water is at least lukewarm.'

'At this hour of the day, *kyria*, it may even be hot,' Takis assured her graciously.

'In that case, I'll have one as well,' Gemma said.

But once in her room, she made no immediate attempt to use the miniscule shower cubicle attached to it.

Instead, she sat on the edge of the rather hard mattress and read Mike's note again. It was odd, she thought, and totally unlike his usual breezy scrawls, and it made her uneasy.

She uttered an impatient exclamation, and got to her feet. Instead of inventing problems, she should be thankful that Mike had taken the trouble to type, rather than expecting her to decipher his normal hieroglyphics.

It was the events of the day which had made her uneasy, and nothing to do with Mike at all. He was probably hale and hearty, and far too interested in his plants to spare her more than a passing thought. And if she was to mention when she saw him that his note hadn't been very welcoming, he would simply look injured and say, 'Well, I told you how to get here, didn't I?'

She sighed, and began to unbutton her dress. If she showered quickly, she would have time to do her packing before dinner, as James and Hilary would probably want to make an early start in the morning.

She was glad she was going to Loussenas with them, and not some unknown driver, she told herself.

And tried to suppress the thought that, fond as she was of Mike, she would far sooner be going to Chania tomorrow than the Villa Ione.

CHAPTER TWO

GEMMA had the same feeling, but doubled and re-doubled in spades, the following day as she stood beside the battered signpost stating Loussenas was one kilometre away, watching James reverse the car with infinite care.

They'd wanted to drive her to the door, but she wouldn't allow it. The road was getting steeper all the time, and deteriorating at every yard into a lacework of potholes. They'd been climbing, it seemed, since the moment they'd left the main road. At first, it had been easy to admire the scenery, but as the road narrowed, and hair-pinned, they all became very quiet, and started averting their gazes from the sheer drop only a foot or two from the car wheels.

Gemma found herself wondering all the time what they would do if they met another vehicle coming down, but by some miracle that problem did not arise.

The little hamlets they passed through, each with its gleaming church, were a relief. They'd stopped in one and drunk lemonade under the awning of a taverna, telling each other that Loussenas couldn't be much further now, although the truth was they had no idea how far it was. They'd asked Takis, but he'd only given the map a cursory glance, stabbed it with his finger and said, 'Loussenas is somewhere above here.' And that, it turned out, had been putting it mildly.

So when they reached the signpost, Gemma had insisted on getting out. The road was

22

slightly wider just here, sufficient to turn the car anyway.

'I really don't like leaving you.' Hilary had peered at her worriedly. 'If Mike is as absent-minded as you say, he might have forgotten you and gone off somewhere, and then where will you be?'

'Stuck,' Gemma returned robustly. 'But it won't happen. He's living at this villa, after all, so someone will be expecting me.'

Hilary looked unconsoled. 'If only we knew where we were staying tonight, or if the villa had a phone, we could keep in touch,' she wailed. 'It's so wild up here. God knows how many thousands of feet we are above sea level. Much higher, and we'd need oxygen.'

'Understating the case as always,' James said wryly. His fingers closed warmly round Gemma's wrist. 'When we get to Chania, we're hoping to stay at the Hotel Dionysius. If anything goes wrong, leave a message, and we'll get back somehow and take you off this bloody mountain.' He paused. 'And you have our address in England, so whatever happens, we want to know how this little adventure turns out.'

They drove off, Hilary waving frantically. Gemma waved back until the car rounded the first bend and vanished from sight. As she started up the road towards the village, she could still hear the sound of the engine growing fainter and fainter, until at last there was nothing but her own footsteps.

In fact, no sign of life but herself, plodding up the road, and a large bird that might have been a buzzard wheeling and circling against the faultless arc of the sky.

She sighed and transferred her case to her other

hand. It was hardly the hilarious reunion she'd envisaged.

She didn't hurry, but she was tired and breathless by the time she reached the first houses. About half a mile earlier, the ground had levelled out into a small plateau. The land had been cultivated, and there was a little cluster of windmills, their sails turning gently in the breeze. Two women were working in one of the fields, black-clad, with the familiar head scarves round their hair and faces, but they didn't look up or make any sign as Gemma passed, and she found this odd. In every other village they'd passed through in the car that day, there'd been waves and smiles from almost everyone, from the bearded priest to the smallest toddler.

A donkey was grazing a small patch of scrub at the side of the road, and it turned its head, fixing her with its mild, incurious gaze as she walked past. Further on, goats were tethered, and bee skeps droned sleepily on a wide ledge.

The village road was now a track, its stones cutting uncomfortably through the thin soles of her sandals. It was little wonder so many Cretans wore boots, she thought ironically.

She put down her case and looked about her, flexing her tired hand. All she could see were village houses, many of them single-roomed by the look of them, and hardly likely to qualify as villas. The doorways were dark, and the window shutters closed, like so many blank eyes staring at her, she thought with a little shiver.

And there was no one about. The place was deserted. There was a tiny kafeneion, but there were no men sitting at its tables in the shade, drinking coffee, and arguing about politics. Each house had its own verandah, but there were no women gathered in groups to chatter and weave the rugs and linens for which Cretans were famous.

Many of the villages they'd passed through had stalls beside the road, displaying their weaving and embroidery, but presumably Loussenas attracted too few tourists to bother.

The Villa Ione couldn't be far away in any direction, but Gemma wished there could be just one friendly face to ask, if only to dispel this growing sense of uneasy isolation which was pressing down on her.

The Cretans were among the most hospitable people on earth. Love for the stranger in their midst was bred into them. She remembered Takis warning them all that if they were offered food and drink anywhere, they should accept, even if they suspected it was all the host possessed. To refuse, he said, was hurtful, and damaging to Cretan pride.

The villagers of Loussenas, Gemma thought wryly, must be the exceptions to that rule. There were people in the houses, she was sure. She could sense movement in the shadowy interiors, but it was clear no one intended to welcome her, or offer as much as a drink of water, even though the well was there, at the end of the street, and a stone's throw from the bright blue door of the little church.

There was nothing for it, but to go on.

Again, she had the feeling that she was being watched. She groaned inwardly. Why had she had to come all the way to Crete simply to discover she was paranoid?

Beyond the church was the priest's house, and beyond that again the ground rose, and through a clump of straggling trees, she saw a high white wall.

Standing in its own grounds, she thought, this desirable residence must be the Villa Ione.

There was a narrow gate in the wall, and a copper bell hanging beside it. The sound was sweet and pure as she rang it, and it echoed endlessly into the stillness, but at last there was nothing left but silence.

Gemma sighed. '"'Is there anybody there?' said the Traveller",' she muttered, and tried the gate. It opened with a faint squeak to the first pressure of her hand, and she stepped inside.

The garden was quite small, but it was well-tended and bright with flowers. The house itself was a good size, the living quarters built over what Gemma assumed had once been a byre and would now be a garage, with a flight of steep steps leading up the side of the building to the terraced entrance. The steps were worn, but in good order, and the whole house looked as if it had just been freshly painted white. Gemma, looking up, saw solar heating panels in the roof. Loussenas might be a backwater, but one of its residents knew about modern technology, it seemed.

There were some Greek letters carved into the stonework at the bottom of the steps, and she peered at them, wishing she'd taken the trouble to learn the alphabet before she came. They looked as if they might spell 'Ione' she decided, and started up the steps.

The little terrace was tiled in a warm terracotta shade, and tubs and urns of geraniums and cyclamen had been arranged round its edge. Splashes on the tiles indicated that someone had been busy with a watering can not long before, and her spirits rose.

She went to the open door, and called a tentative, 'Hello.'

Nothing. No voice, no step, just silence.

Out of the corner of her eye, Gemma caught a faint movement. She swung round, and saw a cat peering at her round one of the urns. It was a typically scrawny specimen, grey and white, and striped like a zebra, with eyes that looked almost twice the size of its pointed face.

Gemma crouched down, and snapped her fingers gently. 'Are you the welcoming committee?'

The cat arched its back as if offended by the suggestion, and vanished in one sinuous movement.

Gemma shrugged and rose to her feet. 'That figures,' she muttered aloud.

She stepped over the threshold, and looked around. She seemed to be in the main room of the house. It was large and airy, and windows, which she suspected were a recent addition, filled the far wall, giving a spectacular view of the valley beneath. The furniture was wooden, and simply designed, and the cushions, rugs and hangings were all hand-woven. One rug, a sunburst in shades of crimson and gold, had been used dramatically as a wall hanging. An archway led through into a small dining room, and beyond this was the kitchen.

It was clean, but very simple with few concessions to modernity apart from the small sink unit, and a tiny refrigerator and cooker, both run off bottled gas she noticed.

There were lamps in all the rooms, suggesting that the Villa Ione had no electricity, and there was no sign of a telephone.

There was a scrubbed wooden table in the middle of the kitchen, and in its centre, a folded sheet of paper anchored by a pottery candleholder.

She picked it up and opened it out. Five typed words. 'Make yourself at home, Gemma.'

'Oh, thank you, I will,' she said ironically. 'I will also have to stop talking to myself, or it could become a nasty habit.'

She opened the fridge. It might be small, but the interior was crammed with food, while the bottom shelf, she was relieved to see, was devoted to cans of beer and soft drinks. She opened a Coke and drank it gratefully, straight from the can.

She kicked off her sandals and wandered back to the living room, enjoying the cool feel of the tiles under her burning feet.

In a way, she could understand why Mike preferred to remain holed up here, rather than submit to the noise and bustle of Heraklion. She perched on the wooden arm of the sofa and stared through the window, wondering which of the stark-looking crags her brother was scrambling about on, looking for specimens, and wishing that just for once he'd given up the hunt to be there to meet her.

Still clutching her can of Coke, she climbed the flight of wooden stairs leading out of the living room to the next floor. Straight ahead of her, a narrow passage led to glazed doors opening on to another terrace, equipped with sun loungers. Two large bedrooms, each with its own small bathroom, flanked the passage, again very simply furnished. Each room contained little more than a double bed, built on to a stone platform in a corner of the room, a large chest of drawers, and an alcove with a hanging rail behind a woven curtain, which presumably acted as the wardrobe. In addition, each room had its own small balcony.

One room was clearly in use already, and in the other the bed had been freshly made up with an attractive blue-and-white bedcover in a Cretan design.

Gemma fetched up her case, and extracted her toilet bag. There were towels, thick and soft and smelling of herbs, folded on a chair, inviting her to make use of them. Well, she thought, with a mental shrug, she'd been told to make herself at home, and she could think of nothing more homely than a shower. She felt hot, tired and sticky, and a little depressed, and showering would refresh her as well as helping to pass the time.

If there was no electricity, perhaps there was no piped water either, and the expensive bathroom fittings were just for show, she thought with a little grimace as she fiddled with the controls of the shower.

But water there was in abundance, and at just the right temperature, she realised with satisfaction, revelling in the sensation as it cascaded through her hair and down her body. It was wonderful to feel the tension seeping out of her, she thought, turning off the water and languidly wringing the excess moisture out of her thick rope of blonde hair. She took one of the towels and wrapped it round herself, sarong-style, anchoring the free end securely. She couldn't use her hand-drier, but she could dry her hair just as well in the sun, and the little terrace at the end of the passage was sufficiently secluded to preclude her needing to get dressed again just yet. If there was nothing else to do, she could always work on her suntan.

She collected one of the paperback novels from her case that she hadn't even started on so far, and padded along to the terrace.

The view from here was fantastic too, the rocky peaks around and above her gleaming white and silver in the sun, but shimmering into a blue and violet haze in the distance. Away down to the right in the valley, she could see the muted sheen of olive groves, interspersed with terraced areas of cultivation, and the harsher green of cypress and scrub. It was a bleak landscape in many ways, but dazzling too.

Everywhere on Crete you were aware of the mountains. The God Zeus had been born in them, although there was some dispute about the actual location. Each peak, each cave had its own myth, its own mystery, and closer to her own times, Gemma recalled, the mountains had provided shelter not only for newborn gods from murderous fathers, but for ordinary mortals—Cretan partisans and their British comrades-in-arms in the last war.

Gemma had hoped to climb up to the cave on Dicte where Zeus was said to have been suckled by the goat Capricorn. She'd thought Mike might take her there. He wouldn't be interested in the myths, but he could look for dittany and other herbs while she looked at the cave, or so she'd reasoned, but she hadn't bargained for the fact that he was living in such a remote place.

She would come back, she knew suddenly, probably next year, and explore all the places she hadn't yet seen. Crete was in her blood already, as she'd somehow always expected it could be. Given a few days, she supposed she might even get to love this uncharacteristic, unfriendly little village. Perhaps its very remoteness had made the inhabitants suspicious of outsiders—and yet, and yet all the stories she'd heard other tourists tell suggested just the opposite. One couple at the hotel in Heraklion had got lost on a moped trip, ending up in a village that seemed at the back of beyond and further. The villagers had feasted them royally, and driven them ceremoniously, moped and all in someone's truck, back to the nearest main road, refusing all offers of payment with smiling dignity.

She sighed. It made the attitude of the inhabitants at Loussenas all the more difficult to understand. But perhaps her imagination was playing tricks again. Maybe those houses had been empty after all, and all the villagers had gone off to market or somewhere, on the one bus a week Mike had mentioned. He would explain when he arrived, she told herself drowsily.

Even in the shade, the terrace was blissfully hot, and the lounger she was occupying the most comfortable place in the world. Every time she looked at the printed page of her book, the words seemed to dance oddly, and it was much easier to let it drop to the floor beside her, and think of nothing except how warm she felt, how relaxed . . .

Too warm, and too relaxed to be struggling up this rocky path which got steeper and more difficult with every step she took, but at the top was the cave she was searching for, the pinnacle of all her dreams in some mysterious way, so she had to keep going.

The cave entrance reared up in front of her, as high and wide as a palace gate, and for a moment she hesitated, peering through the darkness. She wanted to turn and run, but instead, she found her feet carrying her forward. And the cave wasn't as dark as she'd thought at first. There were wall torches flaring every few yards, just as there would have been at Knossos, and she thought 'I must tell Hilary.'

She was excited and frightened at one and the same moment, and the light was almost glaring now, it was so bright, and the only darkness was the man's tall figure, waiting for her, commanding her, drawing her to him. She was close to him now, close enough to feel his hands closing on her, his breath warm on her face, and she looked up and felt the scream rising in her throat as she saw for the first time the great golden bull's mask which hid his face . . .

Gemma sat up with a strangled gasp, staring round her, trying to orientate herself. She must have been asleep for some time, because the sun had moved round, and her struggles had been real because the towel had become unfastened and slid down to her hips. She made a face and stood up, securing it again. It was just as well there was no one around to see her, she thought, and time she got dressed again anyway.

It was then that she heard it—the unmistakable slam of a car door near at hand, and footsteps somewhere below. She almost sagged with relief. Mike, she thought. At last.

The terrace door was closed and she thought, 'That's odd because I left it open . . .' but it wasn't really important. She flew along the passage and down the stairs, almost jumping the last few in her eagerness.

She began teasingly, 'And about time too . . .' then stopped dead, words and movement halting in the same astonished second.

She knew him at once. It was the stranger from Knossos, but looking very different from the sophisticated Western guise of the previous day. No expensive knitted casual shirt, or elegantly tailored cream pants today, but what looked like full Cretan dress from the soft leather knee boots to the dark red embroidered jacket, and the sash enfolding his waist. Only the black headscarf was missing. He'd left the thick dark hair which clustered, curling, close to his head, uncovered.

For a dazed moment, Gemma thought she was still in the middle of that strange dream, then she felt the solid curve of the newel post under her hand, and knew that it was all only too real.

She said, 'What are you doing here?' And what would she do, she asked herself, if he didn't speak English?

Only it seemed that he did.

'Waiting for you,' he said, adding with soft deliberation. 'To awaken.'

Helpless, humiliated colour flooded her face as she assimilated what he had said. He'd seen her on the terrace, asleep and half-naked, and he was letting her know it.

'Why do you blush?' came the cynical question, cutting across her embarrassed silence. 'Your compatriots show as much of their bodies on our beaches every day.'

'Perhaps, but I don't,' Gemma said tightly. 'And what gives you the right to walk in here and spy on me?'

'The right of ownership,' he drawled. 'This house belongs to me.'

Gemma's lips parted but no sound emerged. She stared at him, utterly appalled. 'My God—then—there's been the most terrible mistake. You see, I thought this was the Villa Ione . . .' She stopped abruptly, her forehead creasing. 'But it must be—or how would there have been that note?'

'It is the Villa Ione.'

She stared at him, still frowning. 'Then you must know Mike. Do you know where he is—when he'll be back. He can explain everything . . .'

'That I would doubt.' His voice was even, but there was an underlying coldness which worried her. 'I do not know where this—Michalis is, but

my information is that he left the island—several
weeks ago.'

'Left?' Gemma repeated stupidly. 'But that can't
be true. He's here. He wrote me that note—two
notes. I can show you.'

He shook his head. 'Do not put yourself to such
trouble, Kyria Barton. I wrote those notes.'

There was something terribly wrong. Her whole
body felt as taut as a bowstring. She said thinly,
'You did? But why?'

He shrugged. 'To make sure that you would
come here, *thespinis*, why else?'

'You knew I was coming?' Gemma felt her way
carefully. 'Then Mike must have told you . . .'

'He has told me nothing. How could he when I
have never met him? But he left the letter you
wrote him from England in the room he was
using.'

'And you read it? A personal letter addressed
to someone else?' Her breathing was fierce. 'This
may be your home, *kyrie*, but that's utterly
despicable.'

He was unmoved. 'You have a saying I
believe—that the end justifies the means.'

'Well, I don't happen to believe that,' Gemma
said tautly. 'I don't know what the mistake is, but
there's obviously been one. I'll get my things and
leave at once.'

She turned and went swiftly back up the stairs
to the room she'd thought was hers. Her case had
gone from the floor. For a moment she stared at
the space it should have occupied, then she ran
across to the bathroom and looked inside. The
clothes she had discarded before her shower were
missing too, although her toilet bag was still there.

She flew back into the bedroom. He had
followed her upstairs, and was standing in the

doorway, leaning almost negligently against the jamb.

She said, 'My case—all my things—they've gone. Someone's stolen them.'

'They have not been stolen,' he said. 'They are quite safe and will eventually be returned to you.'

'Eventually,' she repeated almost hysterically. 'But that's nonsense. I want to leave right now.'

He shrugged again. 'I regret that will not be possible.'

There was another silence. Her mind worked feverishly, discovering and rejecting possibilities. She said, 'If you intend to hold me to ransom, then you're wasting your time. I work for my living, but I have no spare cash, and neither does my family.'

For the first time, he looked faintly amused. 'I do not need your money.'

It was hardly likely that he would, she thought bleakly, remembering that car, the designer clothes, the thin gold wristwatch he'd been wearing the previous day. Now, he might look like a peasant, but his voice was educated, and his English superb.

She said slowly, 'Then what do you want?'

'The payment of a debt.' His voice was laconic.

She was utterly bewildered. He'd just said it wasn't money . . .

'Did Mike go off owing you rent? Is that what you mean by debt? Well, I can understand your annoyance, but I'm sure it's just an oversight. You said yourself that Mike had left some things behind, so it's obvious he intends to come back, and settle things for himself.'

'I hope that he does,' he said softly. 'In fact, *thespinis*, I am counting on it.'

She felt cold. She resisted the impulse to hug her

arms round her body in case she betrayed to this man how frightened she was.

She said, 'You may be prepared to wait around for him, *kyrie*, but I'm not. You had no right to ask me here under false pretences. I only have a limited time on Crete and I'm anxious to make the most of it. I'd like my things back now, and directions to the nearest telephone please.'

'And who would you telephone?' The amusement was deepening, she could feel it.

'The friends who brought me here,' she said clearly. 'They offered to come and fetch me if anything went wrong.'

'Then it is unfortunate that you will not be able to make contact with them.'

'But I know where they're going to stay,' she protested. 'All I need is a telephone, and there must be one in the village, if there isn't one here.'

'Yes, there's a telephone in the village,' he admitted almost casually. 'But it is of no consequence, Kyria Barton, as you would not be permitted to make use of it.'

She glared at him. 'And just who would stop me?'

'I would,' he said. 'And so would the people in the village. You see, *thespinis*, they also wish you to stay. To repay in some small measure the heavy debt your Michalis has incurred among them.' He paused. 'How much do you love him?'

She was tempted to reply, 'When he involves me in situations like this—not at all,' but she knew instinctively this wasn't a moment for flippancy.

And how could she describe to this intimidating stranger the kind of exasperated fondness that she normally experienced for Mike? How could she explain that her main reason for seeking him out was to put her mother's mind at rest? She could only be thankful that her mother was hundreds of miles away, and would never know that Mike seemed to be in real trouble at last.

She said with a calmness she didn't feel. 'Enough.'

His eyebrows rose. 'So lukewarm? And yet you came all this way just to be with him.'

'I came all this way to have a holiday. Visiting Mike was intended to be a fringe benefit—a minor one,' she said, adding, 'Not that it's any damned business of yours.'

He looked grimly at her. 'It is my business, *thespinis*, at this moment to discover the depth of your feeling for this man, and his for you.'

Gemma gasped. 'We're brother and sister for God's sake. How do you expect us to feel about each other?' she demanded indignantly.

His dark brows snapped together thunderously. 'What is this story?' he asked contemptuously. 'His name is Leslie, and yours is Barton.'

Gemma sighed. 'He's my half-brother. My mother was married before, but her first husband was killed in an accident at work.' It killed her to have to explain a syllable to this swine, but she would recount her entire family history if it would only get her out of here. 'A year or so later, she met my father and married him, but Mike kept his own father's surname. Now, do you see and now will you let me go?'

He said silkily, 'After what you have just told me, *thespinis*? It makes my reasons for keeping you here doubly potent, believe me.'

She felt incredibly weary suddenly. She said, 'I might, *kyrie*, if I knew what those reasons were. As it is, I'm tired and fed up with the whole affair. I don't know what Mike's supposed to have done, but whatever it is, I'm not responsible for it.'

'I will tell you what he has done,' he said gently. 'He has seduced a girl from this village, abused the trust that was placed in him, and the hospitality he was shown.'

Gemma's lips parted in disbelief. She said angrily, 'There isn't a word of truth in it. Mike wouldn't do such a thing. He's not that sort of person.'

'He is not completely a man—is that what you're saying?'

'No,' she denied furiously. 'But he's no womaniser and never has been. He has a girl in England, but it isn't a serious relationship. I—I'm sure they don't sleep together,' she added, annoyed at having to discuss such a subject with a stranger.

'Then he should have treated Maria with equal honour.' His voice was chilling. 'Your defence of your brother is natural, *thespinis*, but it does not impress me. Maria is to have his child.'

Gemma heard him with dismay. In the books she'd been reading before she came away, she'd learned that on many of the islands the old ways still prevailed, and that a woman's honour was sacrosanct, especially before she was married. She could imagine the kind of slur illegitimacy would confer in this kind of tightly knit community.

She bit her lip. 'Has she said so—accused him?'

'Not at first,' he said grimly. 'But ultimately she confessed everything. How they had met in Chania when she was there working in her uncle's hotel, how she suggested he should use the villa as a base for his work, and brought him here. No one thought wrong of it. The villa was unoccupied, after all, and he made himself popular in the village. Maria's mother came each day to cook and clean for him, until she fell and hurt her leg and the doctor said she must rest.' He paused. 'So

Maria took over her duties. Her family did not wish it. A marriage had been arranged for her with the son of the headman of the next village, and Maria should have been occupied in learning from her mother how to be a good wife. Already her groom's family had been displeased because she had worked for a while in Chania, and had demanded more dowry.' His eyes were like obsidian, dark and menacing. 'They were right to question. Maria had taken your brother as her lover in Chania, and he had persuaded her to bring him here so they could continue the affair in secret.' He shrugged. 'Who knows—perhaps she thought this Michalis would marry her. She knows better now. He has gone, and her bridegroom and his family have repudiated her. She is ruined, and the honour of her family and her village is tainted.'

'But you don't believe that, surely?' Gemma appealed. 'You're a man of the world—you know how things are.'

He said quietly, 'Perhaps, but the people of this village do not. My father was born in this house. He and Stavros were friends, and he was godfather to all his children—Maria too. My father is dead now, and I am head of my family, so in his trouble, Stavros and his kin look to me.'

'But I don't understand what you can do,' Gemma protested. 'I'm sure it's a terrible thing for them all, but you haven't heard Michael's side yet.'

'No,' he said. 'Because as soon as Maria told him there was to be a child, he ran away. He knew, your brother, what Stavros and his sons would do to him if they caught him. But they still seek vengeance.' He paused again. 'And that is why, sister of Michalis, you are here.'

'But I can't do anything.' She spread her hands in appeal. 'If the baby is Michael's, then I'm sure my family will help in some way—with money, of course, or helping Maria make a fresh start where things aren't quite so—rigid.'

'No.' He shook his head. 'Whatever her fault, Maria is our own, and will be protected by us. Yes, you will pay, my girl, for what your brother has done, but not in cash. You will pay in kind— in shame, and your family's shame. You will stay here and work in this house as my servant, as Maria worked for your brother, and I shall take you as and when I please, as he took her.'

His voice deepened, driving the bitter words like sharp nails into her bewildered mind. 'This is my revenge, *thespinis*, for your brother—for your family—to know what it is like to have a beloved child despoiled, taken for pleasure by a man who has no intention of marriage. Perhaps in turn they will also suffer the knowledge that she too carries a child of an alien race in her body.'

CHAPTER THREE

SHE stood very still. There was silence in the room, and he seemed suddenly to have receded to a great distance. She wondered detachedly whether she might be going to faint. She hoped she might die. She hoped anything might happen to her except the kind of horror he was threatening.

Stay calm, she adjured herself frantically. Keep talking—reason with him—don't let him see you're on your knees, because there has to be a way out of this.

She said in a voice she barely recognised as her own, 'I think I've heard enough. I don't know whether this whole thing is meant to be some kind of ghastly joke, *kyrie*, but if so it's in the poorest taste.' She paused. 'And if you wanted to scare me and upset me, then you've succeeded. But that's as far as it goes. If Mike has really caused all this havoc, then he must sort it out for himself. I sympathise, but I'm not getting involved, and I'm certainly not staying in this house on any terms whatsoever.'

'Bravely spoken,' he approved sardonically. 'But the choice is not yours. I thought I had made that clear.'

'But you can't keep me here against my will.' By a superhuman effort she kept her tone level. 'I should run away.'

He looked at her mockingly. 'In this climate, *thespinis*? And naked and barefoot. I don't think so.'

She began, 'But I'm not naked...' then

41

stopped, as she read the message in his dark gaze. She stepped backwards, clutching defensively at the towel. 'You wouldn't.'

'I advise you not to put it to the test,' he said. 'Besides, where would you run to—the village? They would send you back.'

'But they can't be the only people around. There's a bus and . . .' her voice tailed off as she saw his mouth twist derisively.

'The bus called yesterday, *thespinis*. It will not be here again for a week.' He shrugged. 'Who knows—perhaps by that time I will have had enough of you anyway.'

'And I've had enough of you now,' Gemma flared at him. 'You must be out of your mind to threaten me like this. You can't really imagine I'm going to hang around here so that you can—rape me.'

'I have no intention of raping you, *thespinis*,' he said gently. 'I shall use no more force towards you than your brother did to Maria,' he added huskily.

She swallowed. For one terrible moment, she'd had an image of those firm lips crushing hers, parting them—the lean, brown hands caressing and intimate.

She said on a whisper, 'Touch me and I'll kill you.'

He laughed. 'You have spirit. I approve of that. Our time together should prove more pleasurable than I anticipated.'

'There'll be no time together.' Gemma closed her eyes wearily. 'If you do any of the things you've threatened, then I shall go to the authorities. You can't hope to get away with it. We're not living in the Dark Ages.'

'And what will you tell these authorities? That

you went to Knossos and picked up a rich Greek
for a little adventure, and found you were out of
your depth? Because that is what I will tell them.
And the waiter in the taverna will confirm my
story. He saw us watching each other, and he
believes your hurried departure was only to lure
me on. He told me I was a fortunate man, and
wished me well,' he added.

'How nice for you,' she flashed. 'Perhaps if he'd
known what you really intended, he'd have told
you that you were off your head.'

'Perhaps,' he smiled a little grimly. 'But we shall
never know.'

'Why were you at Knossos anyway?' Curiosity
got the better of her.

'I needed to see you before I put my plan into
operation. When I rang the hotel and was told you
were catching a bus to Knossos, I decided to
follow. The hotel said—two English girls travelling
together. You were not hard to pick out.' He
paused. 'And then, your companion called you
Gemma, and I was sure.'

Shakily, she remembered the photograph, and
the waves of burning anger reaching her.

'Wasn't the trip a little unnecessary,' she asked
coldly. 'As you'd apparently already made up your
mind what you were going to do.'

'Ah,' he said softly. 'But you might have been
ugly or undesirable.'

She swallowed, 'And if I had been, you'd have—
changed your plan?' Her voice shook. 'My God, I
wish I had a harelip, a hunchback and a squint.'

'Such a combination might have given me
pause,' he admitted mockingly. 'As it is——' His
eyes went over her again, stripping, assessing,
while the angry colour flared in her face. 'As it is, I
have little to complain about. You are a little

skinny for my taste, but in a situation like ours, one cannot have everything.'

She was mute with rage and humiliation, her hands curling instinctively into claws at her side, a movement which was not lost on him.

He smiled faintly. 'Scratch me in passion, little cat, but not in anger, or you will be sorry.' He pulled back the cuff of his full-sleeved white shirt and examined his watch. 'It is time you began your duties.' He saw her flinch slightly and laughed out loud. 'No, not that. My needs at this moment are a little more prosaic. You may cook me a meal.'

She said steadily, 'I'll see you in hell first.'

He lifted one shoulder negligently. 'As you wish. But you should consider—if you do not cook, then you also do not eat.' He glanced around him. 'It is a pleasant room, *ne*, but I think you would soon grow tired of its four walls.'

And he meant it, she recognised bitterly. She glared at him. 'How do you know I can cook?'

'I don't require gourmet food. There is a leg of lamb to roast, and a salad to make. You should be capable of that at least.'

She was capable of that, and more. She'd been well taught at home, but that was no reason why this—this bastard should benefit from her skill.

She lifted an indifferent shoulder. 'I'll try, but I hope you won't blame me if it's ruined.'

'I hope I shall not have to,' he said quite gently, but there was a warning implicit in his words. He turned and walked away, and she heard him go down the stairs, leaving her alone.

Gemma drew a deep breath and sank down on the edge of the bed. She was trembling violently inside, and her heart was pounding as if it threatened to break through her breastbone.

She bent her head, staring at the tiled floor, and began to breathe deeply and rhythmically, deliberately calming herself. At the moment, she was vulnerable, totally on the run, but that could change, and she could change it.

She began to think. The first sign she'd had that she was not alone had been the slamming of some vehicle's door. Had he really brought that fantastic car all the way up those appalling mountain roads, she wondered incredulously. But if he had, then it was parked near at hand, and that meant that the keys weren't far away either. He was probably carrying them on him, she decided judiciously, and once he was asleep, she could go through his pockets and find them. She tried not to contemplate what it would be like driving an unfamiliar vehicle in bare feet down that snake of a road. She also tried not to think about the events which might precede his falling asleep, because if she did so, then her courage might evaporate entirely.

She sank her teeth into her soft lower lip until she tasted blood. Oh God! Why hadn't she obeyed her first instinct and gone with James and Hilary? She would have been safe then—or would he still have pursued her?

She got up and went into the bathroom. She washed her face and hands in cool water, then rewrapped her towel sarong, fastening it firmly with some safety pins from her toilet bag.

If this was all the covering she was to be allowed, then she would make damned sure it was secure, she told herself, flicking her hair back from her face.

The Cretan was lounging on the narrow sofa when she went downstairs, looking through a newspaper, a glass of ouzo at his elbow. He didn't even glance up at her as she walked through the living room, and out into the kitchen.

Presumably, Gemma thought bitterly, he was used to a woman's presence about the place, both in the kitchen and the bedroom.

She managed to light the oven, then found the joint of lamb from the fridge and put it in a roasting pan. After a brief struggle with herself, she added seasoning, and then inserted some slivers of garlic, alternating with sprigs of rosemary she had found growing in a pot on the windowsill, into slits she had cut in the skin. She dribbled olive oil from a jar over the meat and set it to roast.

It was while she was slicing tomatoes for the salad, that she first noticed the knife she was using. An ordinary kitchen knife, but the blade was pointed and sharp, and it was a line of defence she hadn't considered. If only she'd been wearing normal clothing, she could have hidden it somewhere, but a towel had very few hiding places, she thought ruefully. She needed something with long sleeves so that she could slide the handle under the strap of her watch and let the blade rest against her arm.

And she knew with sudden excitement, exactly what she could use. She gave a slow, triumphant smile. Her captor might think he held all the winning cards, but the last trick could be hers, after all.

She'd hoped she could slip upstairs again unnoticed, but when she came back into the living room, he was clearly waiting for her.

He gestured imperatively, indicating the seat beside him. 'Come here, Gemma.' He saw her hesitation, and the dark brows lifted arrogantly. 'Do you intend to make me fetch you?'

No, she didn't, and that was for sure. Fighting down the signs of inner rebellion, she walked over to the sofa and sat down beside him. If ever she'd needed that knife, it was now, and the damned thing was in the kitchen.

'Would you like me to fill the time until supper with some housework, *kyrie*?' she asked coolly. 'Or have you other plans for me?'

He said softly, 'Little wasp. Has no man ever taught you to sweeten your tongue? My plan is that we should talk a little, get to know each other—even . . .' he paused, as if uncertain how to continue.

'You mean you intend to woo me a little?' She put a world of exaggerated surprise into her voice and expression as she faced him. 'But surely that's unnecessary—for what you are planning?'

He looked at her with a glint of anger in his eyes. 'Quite unnecessary. I'd thought only that it might ease the situation for you, perhaps.'

'Nothing,' Gemma said bitingly, 'could ever do that.'

She wished the sofa was bigger. He was resting his arm along the back of it, and his hand was too near her bare shoulder.

'Then that is a pity,' he said. 'I thought, you see, that we might indulge ourselves, you and I, with a little pretence. I thought we might pretend that yesterday at Knossos, I had joined you at your table for lunch, and afterwards driven you and your companion back to Heraklion, and that later you and I had dinner together.' His voice deepened and softened. 'And that when I suggested you might allow me to drive you into the mountains today, you agreed. So that we have spent the whole day alone together, walking and talking, and now we are here—and our meal is cooking, and we both know it is too late for me to take you back to your hotel—and we are content that it is so.' His voice sank almost to a whisper. Gemma felt his fingers on the nape of her neck, under the fall of her hair, stroking her skin softly and sensuously. 'And you are waiting, Gemma *mou*, for me to kiss you.'

He had moved while he was speaking, she realised with a jolt. He was so close to her now that their bodies were almost brushing. If she turned her head even a fraction, then their lips would meet . . .

She had no intention of doing any such thing, of course, only his warm hand smoothing her skin was dangerously, treacherously compelling. She could feel an answering warmth, deep inside her body, an excitement constricting her throat.

She fought it away fiercely. 'Enjoy your egotistical fantasies, *kyrie*,' she said huskily. 'But they don't alter a thing. As it happens, I wouldn't walk to the end of the street with you—in Knossos, or anywhere else. And now, if you'll excuse me, I have potatoes to peel. Your primary requirement is still for food, I understand.'

'At the moment,' he said between his teeth, 'my most crying need is to give you a beating you will always remember. You had better get out of my sight.'

Her impulse was to run like a hare, but she made herself saunter, head held high as if indifferent to the very real threat in his voice.

Once in the kitchen, she sagged against the table with a barely stifled whimper of relief. Just for a moment or two there, it could have been so easy, so fatally easy to let him get to her.

No matter how much she hated him, there was no way she could deny his attraction. Physically, he was one of the most devastating men she had ever seen. He would have turned heads on any street in the world, and under normal circumstances, he wouldn't have given Gemma Barton, with her fair hair, grey-green eyes and chain store clothes a second look.

And no matter how much he might charm her now, no matter how skilfully he might exercise that potent sexuality, that seductive expertise, she couldn't forget that he was taking her only for some twisted motive of revenge.

And that was her safeguard, Gemma realised painfully. Because she was beginning to realise that if this stranger who had forced his way into her life had wanted her—really wanted her—for herself, then she would not have known how to resist him.

Gemma put the final touches to her appearance, and contemplated her reflection with satisfaction.

The towel lay discarded on the bed, and in its place she was wearing one of the Cretan's own shirts which she'd filched from his room. She'd had a quick look for the car keys too while she was there, but hadn't dared spend too long in case he came upstairs and caught her.

It was dark by now, and he'd lit the lamps downstairs, creating little intimate pools of brilliance against the encroaching shadows.

Soft lights, Gemma thought caustically, but at least there'd be no sweet music to accompany them. And no sweet talk either. He'd barely addressed a word to her, except to ask when the meal would be ready.

His shirt was too large for her, of course, but she'd belted it in with a piece of rope she'd found in one of the kitchen drawers, and rolled up the sleeves a little, making sure they still hung down over her wrists, hiding her watchstrap, and the knife now tucked into it. She would have to be careful not to scratch herself on it, but its mere possession gave her new confidence in herself.

If he laid a hand on her now, he could lose it, she told herself defiantly.

She'd managed to take a quick look outside too, and seen that he hadn't brought the sports car, but a small jeep, which might prove more manageable.

She tugged at an errant strand of hair, nervously flicking her tongue over her dry lips, an image of the man lying stabbed and bleeding on the floor while she searched his pockets for the keys taking nervous hold on her mind. Well—if it happened, he'd asked for it, she assured herself.

With one last jittery glance in the mirror, she went slowly downstairs. The living room was empty, but as she paused at the foot of the stairs, he came through from the kitchen, bending a little to negotiate the doorway. He saw her and stopped, his brows snapping together incredulously as he noticed how she was dressed.

Gemma took the initiative. 'I hope you don't object, *kyrie*.' She allowed what was almost a coaxing note to enter her voice, as she circled briefly and gracefully in front of him. 'But I have to wear something—and beggars cannot be choosers.'

'Beggars usually content themselves with something less than my best shirt,' he said coolly. 'But wear it for this evening.' He gave her a thin smile. 'I can always reclaim it later. Now serve me this meal.'

She murmured a meek word of acquiescence and slid past him into the kitchen. It smelled

wonderful, she had to admit, and she had cooked
Lyonnais potatoes and green beans in addition.

She had set a place for him in the dining room,
but had laid her own knife and fork on the kitchen
table. After all, he'd told her she was to work as
his servant, and the hired help wouldn't normally
expect to eat with the master of the house. Besides,
while she was getting dressed, another little
surprise had occurred to her.

She carved the lamb into thick slices and
arranged it on two platters, adding a helping of
beans to each. Then she took her own serving of
the browned and savoury potatoes, before lifting
the top layer of the remainder and adding a hasty
handful of salt. It looked innocently appetising,
but what it would taste like made her eyes water
just to think of it as she added it to his platter.

At the very least, he would complain. At best,
he might actually be ill, she thought vindictively,
and she would be able to protest in wide-eyed
innocence that in England people liked their food
well-seasoned.

When she took his food into the dining room,
he was pouring wine into two glasses.

'You are not hungry?' He looked questioningly,
as she set down the single plate.

'I was going to eat in the kitchen.'

The firm lips tightened. He said coolly, 'No.
You will eat in here at all times. Is that
understood?'

'Perfectly.' Gemma kept her voice expressionless.
She fetched her plate and took the seat opposite,
watching under her lashes as he picked up his fork.

He said, 'You haven't taken much food.'

'I've plenty,' she returned hastily. 'And anyway,
I'm on a diet.'

'Then you should not be. You are already too

thin as I have told you.' Calmly he reached across and swapped her plate for his. 'It looks delicious,' he added, and began to eat.

She could have ground her teeth in disappointment, but she picked up her own fork and began her meal. The lamb was succulent and fragrant with the herbs she had used, and the beans too were perfect, but she was careful to steer clear of the potatoes.

He must know, she thought, but how could he? He'd not been in the kitchen during the dishing-up process.

'You should eat some potato. It is excellent.'

'Potatoes are my least favourite vegetable,' she returned, forking up a gingerly fragment and trying not to wince at the taste.

'And yet you took the trouble to cook them in this special way for me. You are a paragon among women, Gemma *mou*.'

She didn't have to look at him. The note of unholy amusement in his voice was enough. She picked up her wine glass and raised it to her lips, then jerked away, looking at it with acute suspicion. 'What is this?'

He laughed. '*Retsina*. Resinated wine—but a mild one. It is quite safe to drink. I have not doctored it in any way.'

She put down her glass. 'I think I'd prefer water.'

'As you wish.' He wasn't ruffled in the slightest. 'There is bottled water in the refrigerator, although it is safe to drink from the taps.'

When she came back, he had finished and pushed his plate aside and was peeling himself a peach from a bowl of fruit on the table.

She began to clear both plates, and he halted her. 'Do you intend to starve yourself before my eyes? Or are you sulking because your ploy with the food did not work?'

'I don't know what you're talking about,' Gemma lied coldly. 'And if I have no appetite, is it really any wonder? I'm worse than a prisoner here.'

'At least have some fruit.' He pushed the bowl towards her, but she refused with a curt shake of her head. He sighed. 'Gemma, I am not a barbarian. If I promise you that tonight you will sleep alone, will you eat something?'

She gave him a startled look. 'Why should you promise any such thing? And how do I know you'll keep your word anyway—after all the deceptions of the past couple of days?'

'I'll keep my word,' he said. 'And I have my reasons, but I do not mean to share them—or my bed—with you tonight.'

A wild hope was beginning to stir in her. She stared at him. 'How long will this reprieve go on for—a day—a week—longer?'

He shrugged, the dark face enigmatic. 'Until I decide otherwise, Gemma *mou*.'

She swallowed. 'I don't believe that. I think you're having second thoughts. You—you have to be. You've just said yourself that you're not a barbarian—but to keep me here like a slave is—inhuman.' She paused, her wide eyes fixed on his face in passionate appeal. 'Prove you're not a barbarian. Let me go—please.'

He didn't answer, and she went on, her courage rising, 'If you take me back to Heraklion tomorrow, that will be the end of it. I won't tell anyone or go to the police. After all, I don't even know your name.' She moistened dry lips with the tip of her tongue. 'You talked about pretending earlier—well, we can pretend this never happened.

You—you can tell your friends some story—say that I ran away—anything. They'd have to believe you.' She paused again, eagerly scanning his face, his eyes, for some softening, some answering warmth. 'You can't convince me that you really want to be involved in this sordid little vendetta. You don't even belong here. It's not your concern.'

His clenched fist struck the table, making the crockery dance, and Gemma gasped, shrinking back.

'You talk like a fool, *thespinis*. You—from your safe, conventional English town—what do you know of me—of any of us? If you find this affair sordid, then it is a member of your own family who has made it so. If he needed a woman, he should have gone to a brothel, or sought out one of his own countrywomen who understand how such games are played.' His eyes were grim as he surveyed her. 'You think that to be here with me is the worst that could happen? You are wrong. You are lucky that your brother still lives, and you are buying his life, make no mistake about that. Now, do you still want to run away?'

'Yes,' she threw at him recklessly. 'Because I'm not convinced by this—any of it. Mike's been tried and condemned in his absence, without being given the slightest chance to defend himself. And what about this innocent Maria? It doesn't sound to me that she was exactly unwilling. You've said yourself he didn't rape her.'

'It is precisely because of that, he is not a dead man at this moment,' he said. 'And take care how you speak of Maria to me. To us, the innocence of our girls is their protection, and so it should have been to your brother who was accepted as a friend by the village. He was trusted and he betrayed that

trust, and ran away rather than face retribution.'
The firm mouth curled cruelly. 'But you, Gemma
mou, will not run away. You have my guarantee
on that.'

She got to her feet slowly, trembling in every
limb. 'And you have my guarantee that I'll do
anything—anything to get away from you. I loathe
and despise you for doing this to me. And I know
why you're letting me off the hook tonight—
because you're such a bloody egotist you think if
you wait long enough I'll fall into your arms. Well,
forget it. Anything you take from me will be by
force. And rape can't be any worse than the
contamination of having to live under the same
roof with you.'

He stood up too, his chair crashing violently
away. Two long swift strides, and he was round
the table, towering over her. Before she could
move, his hand had hooked into the open neckline
of her shirt, dragging her towards him.

He said between his teeth. 'Your frankness does
you credit. So you can have no objection if we
dispense with one source of contamination at
least.'

His hand moved downwards, freeing the buttons
as it went. His fingers grazed scorchingly against
the soft mound of her breast, and she bit back a
cry, as if his touch had actually branded her flesh.
And knew in that moment, that if she allowed this
to continue, allowed him to strip her as he was
intent on doing, that she would be branded for life
anyway.

Her fingers fumbled wildly under her sleeve,
then the knife was safely in her hand.

She said hoarsely, 'Let me go—don't touch me,
or I'll use this. I swear I will.'

He stepped back, · looking down expressionlessly at the dangerous glitter of the blade between them.

He said, 'Use it then. Do you know how?'

Her fingers clenched round the hilt in an effort to stop their trembling, her breathing constricted, she watched in disbelief as without haste he unfastened his own shirt down to the waist, pulling the material free of his waist sash so that his chest was completely bare.

His skin was smooth and brown, his chest shadowed with body hair growing down to a vee across his flat stomach. Gemma stood as if paralysed, the knife pointing stiffly towards him. Her mouth was dry, her pulses slow and heavy.

He said again, his voice quiet. 'Do you know how?'

His hands reached and took both her wrists, drawing her towards him. He placed her free hand over the strong rib cage, her other hand just beneath, the tip of the blade resting against his skin.

'Strike upwards,' he advised coolly. 'Like this.' The pressure on her wrist increased fractionally, and as if mesmerised, she saw a bright bead of blood appear under the tip of the knife.

She gave a choking, frightened cry and jerked backwards, throwing the knife away, hearing it clatter across the tiled floor.

Her legs buckled and she sank down to her knees, covering her face with her hands, her tortured breathing tearing at her lungs.

His hands were on her, lifting her inexorably to her feet, and she struggled feebly, moaning 'No.'

His hand twisted in her hair, stilling her, imposing a reluctant submission. His dark face seemed to swim in front of hers. She could read the purpose in his eyes, and a cry of protest formed in her taut throat, never to be uttered as his mouth came down, fiercely, ruthlessly on hers.

She couldn't think, or breathe. She wanted to stay totally passive, impervious to any demands he might make of her, but his lips parted hers with a sensual dominance which enforced a response in spite of herself.

As she capitulated, shaking, yielding her mouth to the sweet erotic abandonment of taste and touch, the violence in him gentled. The agonising tug on her hair faded, and his hand slid down to cup the nape of her neck, his fingers working warm and sensuous magic against her skin. His other arm closed round her, drawing her forward until her bared breasts brushed against the warm muscular wall of his chest, her sensitive nipples excited unbearably by the subtle friction of his body against hers.

She'd never been kissed like this before, she realised dazedly. Never been held in such an intimate embrace, and her body's reaction startled and bewildered her.

She could stay in his arms forever, she realised with a shattering sense of shock, if only he would go on kissing her like this, go on exploring every secret her soft mouth had to offer with such heart-stopping completeness.

And when at last he lifted his lips from hers, she felt almost bereft. Her eyelids flickered open, and she stared up at him in utter confusion, the bruised grey-green depths of her eyes betraying her inner turmoil.

His face was taut, cast in lines as harsh as the mountains which surrounded them. For a long moment he looked down into her face, his gaze burning into hers, then his hand slid, unhurrying, the slim curved length of her body, curving with sensuous mastery round the swell of her hip, urging her forward slightly so that their thighs touched, and she was made compellingly aware of the fact that he was deeply and passionately aroused.

Shudderingly, incredulously, she felt her whole inner being clench in response and desire.

And then she was free—no contact between them at all, and she was ashamed to realise that it was he who had stepped away.

He said harshly, 'You had better go to your room, while I am still capable of keeping my word to you.'

She swallowed convulsively, then turned and went away from him towards the stairs. At the archway, she turned and looked back.

He hadn't moved at all. She could see the rapid rise and fall of his bare chest as he fought to control his breathing, and below his ribcage, that tiny smear of blood. Her hand stole up to her throat in shock as she absorbed the full force of everything which had happened between them.

His voice came to her soft and remorseless. He said, 'It will not be rape.'

Gemma gave a small inarticulate cry, and ran from him—up the stairs on legs which threatened to betray her at every step, and into the illusion of safety offered by her room.

CHAPTER FOUR

GEMMA sat for a long time on the edge of her bed, staring blankly into space, trying to come to terms with what had just happened, and failing by a mile.

She could offer neither explanation nor excuse for herself. This was a man she had cause only to hate. A man whose name she did not even know. A man who was using her as the instrument of a vengeance she did not even comprehend.

Why then, in spite of everything, had she fallen into his arms?

For a moment, she'd even had the upper hand, but her own cowardice had let her down. Gemma shivered. She couldn't have killed him, she thought, but she could have hurt him, incapacitated him sufficiently to allow her to make her getaway unmolested. Now she was back to square one, or worse.

She thought her defiance had surprised him, but there would be no element of surprise in future. He would now be prepared—on the watch for anything she might do.

But he had no idea that she could drive, she told herself, trying to rally her spirits. And her next plan had to be to find the keys of the jeep, even though the prospect of having to negotiate that mountain road in an unfamiliar vehicle frankly appalled her.

But what other choice did she have, without shoes to walk in, or indeed, proper clothes?

Once inside the jeep, she reasoned, she would be

safe until she got to Chania. She'd find James and Hilary somehow, and Hilary would lend her anything she needed. She would have to enlist James' good offices over her missing passport and travellers cheques, she realised ruefully, and sighed out loud. God, what a mess it all was.

And when she did get away, there was still the problem of Michael to contend with. Somehow she would have to find him, wherever he'd gone, and warn him to stay out of Crete for good, even if he claimed he was innocent of the accusation. If her unknown captor was right, it would be all too easy for any determined and vengeful persons to stage an accident in these mountains.

She looked at the flickering flame of the little lamp beside her bed, and her lips twisted. She'd found it alight when she came in, and realised that he must have done it while she was occupied in the kitchen. Before, she thought, he'd come to the decision to let her sleep alone that night.

She shivered again. She couldn't count on being allowed another respite, which made her need to escape during the next twenty-four hours not just imperative, but overwhelming.

Those few agonisingly passionate moments in his arms had taught her things about herself that she had never known, could never have guessed. In the past, although she'd had a number of boyfriends, she'd always regarded herself as something of a cool customer. It had always been simple enough to call a halt when more than kisses were sought, and this was why she'd always fought shy of any closer commitment. In a way, she'd almost been afraid that there might be something lacking in her, which would make her a bad bet for any man seeking a normal loving relationship with a wife. So, while the kissing had been enjoyable enough, she'd never been tempted to go further.

Except tonight, she thought, putting tentative fingers against the swollen fullness of her mouth.

Decent men, with perfectly honourable intentions, had wanted her, and she had sent them away without one pang of regret. Why in hell, she asked herself despairingly, had she had to learn her first lesson in desire from a stranger who cared nothing for her, who was only taking her to satisfy some primitive notion of justice?

Yet he himself was far from primitive, she thought wonderingly. He might wear peasant clothing, but everything he had, including the shirt she herself was wearing, was of the finest quality. He was educated and sophisticated—so how could he lend himself to this barbarity?

And all the time, as she sat there, watching the little flame and thinking, she was listening for the moment when he would come upstairs.

He'd promised—but would he keep that promise, she thought, her heart thudding oddly. After all, he'd brought her to the brink of surrender as his own instincts and experience must have told him. Wasn't it more than likely that he might decide to follow up the advantage he'd gained?

And if he came upstairs and saw a light under her door, mightn't that provide the final prompting he needed?

With a burst of nervous energy, Gemma blew out the lamp. Moving quietly in the darkness, she washed her face and cleaned her teeth in the bathroom. The shirt she removed and hung over a chair. It might once again be all she had to wear tomorrow, she thought wryly. She turned back the coverlet to the bottom of the bed, and slipped under the thin sheet, welcoming its fresh coolness against her heated skin.

But she couldn't relax. Tensely she lay looking up at the ceiling, and waiting for what might be.

It wasn't a very big house, and in the quiet night air every little sound seemed magnified. She could hear him moving around downstairs—even, she thought, hear the chink of a bottle on a glass. It sounded as if he was drinking, and she wasn't sure whether this was a good thing or a bad.

And it was while she was trying to decide, that exhaustion finally claimed her, and she fell asleep.

When Gemma awoke, it was early daylight. For a moment, she was totally disorientated, staring round her wondering where she was, then memory came flooding back, and she sank back against the pillow with a little groan.

The events of the past twenty-four hours might just have been some awful dream. Now, she knew, it was all only too real.

She wondered what had woken her. It was at least an hour before she normally stirred. She slid out of bed, and, naked, padded over to the window, opening the shutters a cautious fraction. She could see the road leading down to the village quite plainly, and walking down it, away from the villa, was a girl, dark-haired and wearing a red dress.

As Gemma watched, the girl swung round in her tracks and stared back at the villa. Even from that distance, Gemma could see that she was a vibrantly pretty girl, although her looks were currently marred by a sullen expression, and her shoulders had a dejected droop as she continued to trudge down the track.

Gemma pursed her lips in a silent whistle, then grabbed the shirt from the chair, and thrust her arms into the sleeves, her fingers clumsy with haste as she tried to fasten the buttons. She needed to talk to that girl, and fast.

She let herself quietly out of her room, and slipped stealthily down the stairs.

The sun pouring in through the light curtains illuminated the living room with merciless emphasis. Gemma's nose wrinkled as she surveyed the bottle and used glass which stood by the sofa, the ash tray, overflowing with butts, and the general disarray of cushions and rugs. But she didn't have time to worry about that now, she told herself impatiently, and if she could just talk to that girl for a few moments, she might never have to bother about it at all.

She'd expected to have to wrestle with bolts on the door, but to her surprise it wasn't even locked. She opened it with care, gritting her teeth as the hinges squeaked slightly. Not that it mattered, she thought optimistically. If that bottle was anything to go by, her captor should still be sleeping it off at noon.

'You're going somewhere?'

Gemma almost screamed. Certainly she jumped, whirling round, her heart thudding painfully. And, of course, he wasn't sleeping anything off. He was standing in the archway watching her, hands resting lightly on his hips. He looked the worse for wear, however, his eyes narrowed against the light as if it hurt him, and she hoped that it did. His hair was dishevelled too, and he hadn't shaved.

'I was just letting in some fresh air,' she returned defensively. 'Or perhaps you don't think it's necessary?'

He shrugged as if fresh air or poison gas were all the same to him. 'Do as you wish,' he said flatly. 'And then you may prepare breakfast.

You will find fresh bread in the kitchen,' he added shortly.

'Oh?' Gemma was intrigued in spite of herself. 'How did that get here?'

'One of the villagers brought it.' His tone was impatient. 'Now, if you have no more questions, I will go and finish dressing.'

She said, 'I saw a girl from my window. I thought that perhaps it might be Maria.'

'Then I advise you not to think,' he said unpleasantly. 'Just do as you're bidden. And call me when breakfast is ready,' he flung at her over his shoulder, as he turned towards the stairs.

'Certainly,' Gemma returned coolly. 'And where would you like breakfast—in the dining room—on the terrace?' Or thrown at you, she added silently.

He shrugged again. 'On the terrace will do perfectly well.'

'And when I do call you,' she went on cordially, 'what do I say?'

He frowned. 'What do you mean.'

'Well, I don't know your name,' she said. 'So how do you wish to be addressed. Sir, perhaps? My lord? Your majesty?'

The frown deepened to a scowl. 'I recommend you to guard your tongue, *thespinis*. I am not in the mood for your insolence this morning.'

'So I've noticed,' she returned drily. 'Sexual frustration and a hangover seems to be a lethal mixture.'

His eyes narrowed dangerously. 'What do you dare say to me?'

'Nothing,' Gemma said hastily. 'A little joke, that's all, but out of place. I'm sorry.'

He looked at her for a long, disturbing moment. 'I think you will be,' he said at last, and went upstairs.

Gemma drew a deep breath, and expelled it shakily. She was a fool to provoke him, even mildly, under the circumstances. She would have to keep her natural sense of mischief firmly under control, she decided wryly.

She tidied the living room hastily, clearing away the debris from the previous night, and shaking up the cushions and hanging the rugs to air over the terrace balustrade.

Then she went into the kitchen. The bread was on the table. It was still warm, and it smelled wonderful, Gemma thought ecstatically, as she emptied a carton of orange juice into a jug, and filled a dish from the tin of jam in a cupboard. There was fresh coffee, but she wasn't sure how to make it in the Greek manner, so she compromised with instant.

She carried the tray out to the terrace and set it on the table, covering the food with a cloth as a safeguard against the inquisitive wasps which were already gathering.

Then she went upstairs. Her hand was raised to tap on his door, when it opened suddenly, startling her. Downstairs, he'd been wearing a pair of faded denims and nothing else as far as she was aware, but now he had changed once again into the Cretan dress, minus the jacket he'd been wearing the previous day. He'd shaved, and his hair was wet from the shower, and she could smell the cool, damp fragrance of his skin.

He was one of the most physically arresting men she had ever seen in her life, Gemma thought dazedly, looking at the way in which his damp hair clung curling to the shape of his head, the length of the lashes which shadowed eyes as black as onyx, the sculpturing of that wickedly experienced mouth . . .

She said huskily, 'Your breakfast is ready,' and turned swiftly to escape downstairs, only to be brought to an abrupt halt by his hand on her arm.

He said silkily, 'Perhaps the day should begin here. *Kalimera*, Gemma *mou*.' And bending his head, he brushed his mouth lightly across hers.

As a kiss, it was over almost as soon as it had begun, but it left Gemma with the bruising, shameful knowledge that she had wanted it to go on. Her pulses were pounding, and breathing was suddenly difficult. She did not dare look at him again, merely turning and almost stumbling in her haste to get downstairs.

By the time he joined her on the terrace, she had almost regained what rags of composure were left to her.

His eyes flicked over her, travelling frowningly from her aloof expression to the empty plate in front of her.

He said, 'The bread is good, Gemma. Take some.'

'I'm not hungry,' she informed him defiantly.

'Nevertheless, you must eat, or you will make yourself ill.' There was a steely note in his voice.

Gemma raised her eyebrows. 'Yet only twenty-four hours ago you were threatening to let me starve.'

'It still seems to have much to recommend it,' he said grimly. 'However, I have allowed humanitarian counsels to prevail. Besides,' he added with a shrug, 'a girl weak from hunger is unlikely to prove very stimulating as a companion in bed.'

Gemma's lips tightened. She was incredibly hungry—the sun, the air, the appealing fragrance of the bread all putting an extra edge on to her normally healthy appetite. Now, she was damned if she would eat as much as a crumb in front of him.

She said glacially, 'But then providing you with that kind of entertainment is the last thing I have in mind.'

'So—what is the first?' He sounded politely interested, no more.

'Getting out of here,' she said between her teeth. 'And putting you in jail where you belong.'

'An ambitious scheme.' He didn't sound particularly perturbed. He spread jam on to a slice of bread and ate it with every appearance of enjoyment.

'But not an impossible one.' She hesitated. 'After all, you can't hope to get away with this. I'm not completely alone in the world. I have a return flight to take—a job at home in England— my family. If I don't return when I'm supposed to, then enquiries will be made. You must see that.'

He shrugged, 'And when these enquiries are made, Gemma *mou*, what will be discovered? That you were here with me. That we were lovers. It is a story as old as time, and will surprise no one— except, perhaps, your family, and it is my intention that they should suffer through your dishonour anyway.'

Her voice thickened. 'They don't deserve that.'

'Nor did Stavros and his wife,' he said coldly. 'It is something this brother of yours should have considered before he seduced Maria.'

She lifted her chin. 'So—what would satisfy them? If Mike married her?'

'Do you think that is likely?'

Gemma bit her lip. 'No,' she said honestly after a moment's thought. 'He's still a student. He can't afford to get married to anyone for several years yet. Although I suppose he'll have to contribute

something to the baby's support,' she added
frowning. She was silent for a few moments,
staring down at the empty plate in front of her,
tracing its pattern with her forefinger. Then she
said, her voice unsteady, 'If you're determined to
punish Mike through me, can't you leave it at
that?'

'I'm not sure I understand you.' He drank some
coffee.

The colour deepened painfully in her face. 'If
I—agree to—to let you do what you want to me,
will you let me go afterwards—when it's over?'

His mouth twisted wryly. 'I have had more
beguiling invitations, *matia mou*. Why should I
agree to any such thing?'

'I've told you—I have a life in England to return
to—a career. I want to get back to them,' she said
fiercely.

'And a man too, perhaps?'

The words of denial were already quivering on
her lips, when Gemma scented danger in the
apparently idle question.

She said, 'That's none of your concern.'

'You think not? Yet I am naturally interested to
know whether you will come to me a virgin, or
some other's willing pupil.'

She tried for nonchalance. 'Of course there have
been men.' She shrugged. 'As you've implied
yourself, things are different in England. We—we
don't lead the same sheltered lives as your girls.'

'Is that a fact?' He leaned back in his chair,
surveying her through lazily narrowed eyes. 'But if
you are so free with your favours, Gemma *mou*,
why the virtuous protests?'

Gemma could have ground her teeth in
frustration and temper. She had been certain that
he'd wanted her to admit she was a virgin—that

for some reason, probably to make his revenge totally complete, she supposed bitterly, it was important to him. It had been a long shot, but she'd hoped that if she claimed experience, hinted that he would be one of a long line, he might find it sufficiently distasteful to bring about a change of mind where she was concerned.

She said sharply, 'Because I prefer to have a choice. Having forced me into this situation . . .'

He laughed. 'What force have I used?' he challenged. 'Within the confines of this house you move freely. I have not tied you to my wrist—dragged you screaming into my bed. There are no marks of violence on your skin—no bruises.'

She met his glance defiantly. 'Not yet.'

'Not ever.' He lifted a dismissive hand. 'Why should I use brute strength when I know a little patience will succeed in bringing me everything I desire from you?' His eyes met hers, steadily, unsmilingly. 'As we both know, Gemma *mou*,' he added softly.

The silence between them seemed to crackle. Gemma swallowed quickly. 'You—you revolting egotist,' she said.

His mouth twisted. 'So—if we are calling names—you, my lovely Gemma, are a little hypocrite. At Knossos you were as aware of me as I was of you. I need not have been honest with you. I could have sought your acquaintance, as if you were any pretty tourist to whom I was attracted—could have brought you here, seduced you, taken you body and soul—and then, but only then, told you the truth. It was a temptation, believe me, *matia mou*. Is that what you would have preferred?'

She sat very still, her mind considering and rejecting the all-too potent images his words had conjured up. She could imagine only too well how she'd have felt, falling asleep in his arms, sated with passion, believing herself desired, then waking to the ultimate cruelty of the truth.

It could, she realised stunnedly, have destroyed her—and the shock of that realisation drained the colour from her face. It contained implications she had no wish to explore—implications with the power to terrify her.

From a great distance, she heard him repeat quietly and remorselessly, 'Is that what you would have preferred?'

She said thickly, 'No.'

'That is what I thought.' He sounded as if the question had only been of minor interest to him. He drank the rest of his coffee, and pushed the cup away, glancing at his watch as he did so.

Gemma took herself in hand. 'An appointment?' she asked with heavy sarcasm. 'Please don't let me keep you.'

He smiled thinly at her. 'You could not, Gemma *mou*, if I did not wish to stay. And, as it happens, I do have an appointment—business to attend to elsewhere today. I hope you will not be too lonely.'

She stared at him. 'Oh, I imagine I'll survive.' She spoke calmly, but her heart was beating faster with the first stirrings of excitement. He was actually going to leave her here—alone. Of course, he'd be taking the jeep, she hadn't the slightest doubt about that, but there were other ways—there had to be . . .

'I expect you will.' His smile widened slightly. 'But to ensure it, I have arranged a companion for you.'

The balloon of hope inside her deflated as quickly as if it had been stabbed with a pin. She forced her face and voice to remain impassive.

'You're very thoughtful, *kyrie*. But I really don't need a surrogate jailer.'

'You think not?' He pushed back his chair and got up. 'But you need something, *pedhi mou*, to protect you from the consequences of your own recklessness. And I feel sure that if I left you here, completely alone, you would be tempted to be—very reckless.' He paused. 'As it is,' he added sardonically, 'I can relax and go about my business, knowing that you are here, safely occupied with your domestic concerns. Who knows?' He shrugged slightly. 'You might even miss me a little.'

Her pulses felt erratic. 'I wouldn't count on it.'

'You might also,' he went on silkily, as if he hadn't heard her last remark, 'give some further thought to the fascinating offer of your body you made me earlier.' He paused again. 'I am inclined to accept, so if you were not serious, now is the time to say so.'

'I wasn't serious,' she said.

'Very wise.' He sounded almost approving. 'You see, *agape mou*, I would have guaranteed nothing in return. You assumed, did you not, that I would be satisfied with one brief coupling which you would somehow endure?' He shook his head, smiling faintly. 'You are wrong, my lovely one, on all counts. Once I have you, Gemma, I intend to keep you—for a while at least. And it is also possible that once you belong to me, you will not want to leave either,' he added softly.

She wanted to say something shattering, something which would blast his ego, his self-esteem to smithereens, but no words came. Did he really believe, she found herself wondering shakily, that his physical enthralment of her would be so simple, so effortless as he implied? And knew, in that moment, that he did.

At last she heard herself say in a voice which did not seem to belong to her, 'You're mad—you have to be. It's the only explanation.'

'It's a crazy world, Gemma *mou*.' He paused. 'I will bring food for this evening with me when I come back. Is there anything else you require? Anything you would like me to bring you from the town?'

She raised her eyebrows in exaggerated surprise. 'Trying to buy me now, *kyrie*? Surely you're not losing faith in your own technique at this late stage.'

He looked at her for a long moment, bleakly, and in silence, his mouth firmed to a harsh line. Then he said, 'It was a gesture of goodwill, intended perhaps to ease the situation a little. But forget it.' He shrugged dismissively, and turned away.

Gemma bit her lip. 'I'm sorry,' she said stiffly. 'Actually, there is something—but I'm sure you don't have to go all the way to town for it.' She took a breath. 'I'd like something to wear, please, if only as an alternative to this.' She indicated the shirt, with a gesture of self-derision. 'It surely isn't too much to ask?'

'No.' He went on watching her. 'At least not when it is asked in the right way.'

'I said "please".' Her chin went up.

'I heard you, but I would have preferred the request to be made with a little more warmth.'

'Do you want me to go on my knees?' She fiddled with the dishes, piling them together fussily on the table, avoiding looking at him.

'No.' He paused again. 'I think I would prefer you to kiss me.'

'Go to hell.' Gemma spoke with bitter distinctness.

'As you wish. Then your request is refused.'

She stared down at the table. 'You mean—if I kiss you—and only then—you'll bring me something else to wear.'

'Why, yes, *matia mou*. That is exactly what I mean,' he said mockingly. 'Is it so much to ask?'

She swallowed. 'I'm not actually putting you to any trouble. You've got my luggage hidden somewhere, after all. You only have to open the case . . .'

'And you only have to walk a few paces across this terrace to me,' the tormenting voice returned. 'The decision is yours.'

Head bent, cheeks burning, hating him, she took the requisite number of steps. He didn't move, and she had to stand more or less on tiptoe to reach his olive-skinned cheek with her lips, briefly and awkwardly.

He said something terse and very violent half under his breath, and in his own language. His hands clamped down on her shoulders, forcing her to stay where she was. His eyes glinted down at her contemptuously.

'Is that what you call a kiss, Gemma?' he demanded harshly. His dark face seemed to swim before hers, and she closed her eyes on a little shaken gasp as his mouth fastened on hers, taking expert, insolent toll of its sweetness, his tongue exploring its every contour, every moist crevice. She couldn't speak, or think, or taste anything other than him. He seemed to fill the universe. She felt the deep inner trembling start within her, and knew that without that fierce bruising grip on her shoulders she would have collapsed on to the floor, her legs no longer strong enough to support her.

She was faint, she was going to die. Perhaps she was already dead, and this was Paradise already within her reach. The incoherencies rioted crazily in her head, as the world tilted on its axis dragging her down against the force of gravity into some undreamed-of maelstrom of sensation.

She couldn't breathe, her head was being forced back at an impossible angle, and when he let her go the pain of separation was almost more than she could bear.

She lifted her hand and touched her swollen lips softly with her fingers, staring down at the tiled floor at her feet, watching wild golden particles whirl and dance before her wide and frightened gaze, trying to control the ragged hurry of her breathing, so that he wouldn't know—dear God— what his exquisite brutality had done to her.

'So.' His own breathing didn't sound any too sure. 'Now we begin to understand each other a little.' His hand took her chin, forcing it upwards, making her meet his eyes, darker than night, harder than obsidian. 'Let our Cretan sun warm you, Gemma, before I return tonight.' He added grimly. 'My patience is not endless.'

He let her go, and she twisted past him into the house, through the living quarters and into the kitchen, as if it represented some sanctuary.

But there was no sanctuary, she thought, as she turned on the tap letting the cold stream of water play gratefully over her wrists and hands.

Not even where she most needed one—inside her own heart.

CHAPTER FIVE

IT seemed a very long time before she heard the sound of the jeep starting up and driving away. But then she had spent most of it leaning against the sink unit, praying that he wouldn't follow her. She was on the ropes, confused and vulnerable, with nowhere to run, and nowhere to hide.

She moved at last, slowly and stiffly, as if she wasn't quite sure that her recalcitrant body would obey her, would observe the commands of her brain.

But her brain didn't seem to be functioning any too efficiently or it would have warned her, reminded her just how dangerous it was to provoke him.

She sighed tremulously, letting the tip of her tongue flick along her dry lips, exploring tentatively the slight soreness which still lingered. But that might be the least of her troubles before this long day was over, she thought, wincing.

She sighed again, but more sharply, bracing herself to fight the feeling of inevitability which threatened to overwhelm her.

He had said it would happen, that he would take and she would give, and she knew now how fatally easy it would be to let herself go with the tide, drown with him in sensual oblivion. She had never wanted a man before, and it was a terrible irony that it should be this particular man who was the focus of her first passionate desires.

She wished with all her heart that she really had the experience she'd foolishly boasted of. At least she might know how to cope with what was happening to her. Might be able to judge, to gauge the astonishing intensity of response he seemed able to arouse in her and which nothing in her life so far had prepared her for. She was ashamed of it, but she could no longer deny it existed.

She listened intently for a moment. She'd not heard any other voices, any sounds of movement but his while she'd waited in the kitchen like a cornered animal. Perhaps he'd forgotten to provide her with the alternative jailer he'd threatened her with, she thought hopefully, and if so—if so . . .

She went quickly to the stairs and up them, straight to his room. It would have been nice to have had her own things back to escape in, but under the circumstances she couldn't wait around for them to be returned to her. She would have to make do with whatever she could find.

She pulled back the curtain and scanned the hanging rail. It would have to be another shirt, preferably one even more opaque than the sample she was currently wearing. And not a rope belt either. One of his own sashes from the second drawer in the chest. She'd managed without underwear so far, and supposed she could go on doing so. But shoes of some kind were essential, and not those damned knee boots he favoured. The alternatives seemed to be sandals, or a pair of flat heelless mules. She tried them on. They were far too big, of course, but she thought if she stuffed the toes with paper, she might be able to shuffle along somehow. Anyway, she would try. This was her last chance, and she had to take it.

She changed into the clean shirt, belting it carefully round her slim waist tightly, and

frowning a little as she twisted and turned in front
of the mirror assessing the effect. It was perfectly
decent, just as the other one had been, she
thought, and it was only her own self-consciousness
about her lack of other attire that made her doubt
it. It covered her as adequately as any dress.

The mules were far more of a problem. It took
three-quarters of the Greek newspaper she found
down in the living room to make them stay on at
all, and they felt thoroughly uncomfortable as well
as restricting quite considerably her freedom of
movement. But then, she wasn't planning on
taking part in a hundred metre sprint, she
reminded herself. She wasn't going to hurry at all,
in case anyone was watching her. She was simply
going for a gentle stroll—up the mountain.

She wished she'd paid infinitely more attention
to Takis' map, then she might know if there were
other villages round about. Slightly more civilised
villages, she thought hopefully, where they didn't
conduct weird sexual vendettas . . .

Surely, there had to be something else, and,
eventually, someone else. Someone who would
help her. Loussenas, and its watching, hostile eyes,
couldn't be the end of the line.

She took a deep breath. There was only one way
to find out, she told herself resolutely, and
shuffled, cursing the unwieldy mules silently, to the
door.

For the moment, she thought the low rumbling
sound she heard was distant thunder, and paused,
scanning the cloudless sky with frank dismay. The
last thing she wanted was to be caught in a storm,
next door to naked. She wanted to escape, not die
of pneumonia.

The rumble came again, and she realised with
heart-stopping suddenness that it was emanating,

not from the Lord Zeus' displeasure with mankind, but from the throat of a very large dog.

She stopped dead, staring in dismay, and the dog looked back at her, lifting its upper lip in a snarl which was no more pleasant for being silent.

Gemma said in a voice of false cheerfulness. 'Hello then, boy, Good dog.' She extended a clenched fist for the animal to sniff, a gesture of confidence which it treated with contempt, snarling again, and this time adding sound to the performance. It was stationed slap in the middle of the terrace, and clearly had no intention of budging.

Gemma toyed with the idea of bribing the thing with the remains of last night's leg of lamb, but dismissed it. This particular Cerberus looked as if he meant business, and would require a far more substantial sop to be thrown to him than a few leftovers.

Aloud, she said, 'Cerberus is a good name for you, hell-hound,' and went back into the house. She stood for a few moments, watching the dog choose a patch of shade and lie down in it. But not, it seemed, to sleep. Massive chin on large paws, it lay and gazed towards the house, ears pricking attentively at every move she made.

A companion, she thought corrosively. The half was not told me.

Moving cautiously, the offending mules kicked into a corner, she began to tidy the house, to sweep and dust, to fill the long minutes with the mundane details of domesticity. And the dog Cerberus seemed to track every move she made with his unswerving gaze.

Once, and only once, she made an attempt to get past him to the steps, but he growled at her with such positive venom that she abandoned it almost immediately.

When she went upstairs, he rose, shook himself and padded after her. Gemma found it almost a relief. She'd been trying to gauge the drop from the terrace where she'd sunbathed that first afternoon—could it really be only yesterday? she asked herself in frank astonishment—and the dog's presence meant that she wouldn't even be tempted to try and risk breaking a leg, or worse.

The people who advocated death before dishonour had obviously never actually been faced with the choice, she thought with irony.

The dog lay in the passage and watched her as she moved from one room to the other, tidying bathrooms and straightening beds. As Gemma worked, she chatted to him as if he had been a pet instead of a jailer, and eventually was rewarded by a faint and perfunctory swish of the tail. But that, she thought wryly, was probably as amiable as he was likely to get.

In the Cretan's room she worked slowly, taking the time to look around her, now that the coast was relatively clear.

He was still very much a mystery, and this room—his domain—provided no clues at all. There were his clothes, expensive and of excellent quality as she'd already noted, but few other personal possessions—no photos, letters or papers to give any indication of · his identity. She wondered if that was deliberate—part of the plan—or perfectly usual for the way he lived his life. A man, she thought, who travelled lightly because he travelled alone.

But that, of course, was pure speculation. He probably had a wife and six children somewhere. Perhaps he was with them at this moment, playing the part of the devoted family man, she thought with a little hostile snort.

And if this wife existed—did she know what he was doing in these days away from her? And, if so, would she care? Would her own desire for vengeance align with his, cancelling out all other considerations?

It seemed impossible. What wife could know that her husband was sleeping with another woman, whatever his motive, and endure that knowledge?

I couldn't, Gemma thought fiercely, and found that her hands had involuntarily clenched into fists at the idea.

She gave a small weak laugh. It seemed she was allowing her imagination to run away with her.

Besides, any woman who married a man like that was asking for trouble, and would deserve all she got.

But being in his room like this, she was forced to admit, was a strange sensation. Straightening his bed, shaking up the pillow, folding the linen sheet which was the only covering, was an only too forcible reminder of what the night could bring.

Gemma swallowed thickly. Simply touching the bed which held him seemed to conjure up an image so powerful that she had the odd feeling she had only to turn round, and she would find him there—waiting to take her in his arms, to draw her down beside him on to the bed . . .

The dog barked, gruffly, throatily and Gemma jumped, almost expecting that the Cretan had materialised beside her somehow, and that the dog was giving warning.

But Cerberus' attention had been engaged by something or someone downstairs, and as Gemma paused to listen, she could hear the sound of footsteps moving about, but not, she thought, those of a man.

The dog was already halfway down the stairs and she followed more gingerly. She heard the dog growl, then bark again, and a girl's voice speaking sharply in Greek. The dog's ears went down and his tail wagged. Whatever the girl had said, they were clearly magic words, Gemma thought.

She recognised her at once—it was the girl in the red dress she'd seen earlier, and she still looked sulky, her heavy-lidded dark eyes almost fierce as they met Gemma's.

Gemma said coolly and clearly, 'My name is Gemma Barton, and I think you must be Maria.'

The girl shrugged. She muttered, *'Then katava-leno.'*

Gemma's Greek was minimal, but that was one of the few phrases she'd managed to master. She said sharply, 'I think you understand perfectly well. And don't tell me that you and Mike only spoke Greek to each other because it's just not possible.'

There was a silence. Then the girl said, 'You are the woman of Michalis?'

'His sister,' Gemma corrected. '*Adelphi tou,*' she added for good measure.

'Sister.' The black brows snapped together frowningly. 'I do not understand.'

And Gemma did not feel capable of explaining all over again to someone whose knowledge of her language seemed limited. She sighed.

'Did Mike—Michalis—never mention that he had a sister? Didn't he talk about his family at all?'

Silence. Another shrug. 'A little—maybe. But not a sister.'

'Nevertheless, that's who I am.' Gemma made herself smile, speak pleasantly, and was relieved to see the heavy frown lift a little, the sullen expression lighten.

'You know where Michalis has gone? You can help me?'

'I think I'm the one who needs help,' Gemma told her drily. 'Do you know why I have been brought here?'

The girl nodded. 'It is a punishment, although this was not my wish, you understand,' she added hastily. She put a protective hand on her abdomen in a curiously poignant gesture. 'My father—my brothers were so angry. They threatened many things—bad things.'

Gemma said gently, 'This is also a bad thing, Maria.'

Maria's eyes widened sceptically. 'To be here—with Kyrios Andreas?' She almost giggled. 'There are many—many women who would not think so, *thespinis*. Many who would be glad to take your place.'

'Including yourself?' Gemma asked sharply, irritated by the knowing gleam in Maria's eyes.

The girl drew herself up. When she wasn't scowling, she was incredibly pretty, Gemma thought, her figure full-breasted and voluptuous.

'Not I, *thespinis*.' She shook her head. 'The father of Kyrios Andreas was our *nonos*—our godfather.' She crossed herself. 'In his life, a good man, and important man. Always he was most kind to us. But I was not for his son. Never would my father have dreamed of such a thing. When Kyrios Andreas takes a wife, she will be a woman of wealth and property, as is fitting.'

So—his name is Andreas, and he isn't married, Gemma thought.

She said, 'Maria—whatever wrongs my brother has done you, I can't stay here. You must see that. I'm sure that if he'd known you were pregnant, he'd never have gone off like this and . . .'

'But it was because he knew that he went, *thespinis*.' Maria sounded almost matter-of-fact about it. 'If he had stayed, my father and brothers might have killed him. It was better he went. But he promised he would help, and he will.'

Gemma bit her lip. 'Are you thinking that he'll marry you, perhaps?'

There was a pause, then a negative shake of the head. Maria said flatly, 'It would not be fitting.' She did not meet Gemma's gaze.

She said, 'I don't believe that, Maria, and I know my parents wouldn't either, if you love each other. But there would be problems. Michalis is still studying. He can't afford to get married, for one thing. And how do you suppose he will feel if I'm forced to stay here with—with this—Andreas?'

Maria shrugged. 'As I said, *thespinis*, it was not my will that you should be brought here. I tried to tell them—to speak against it, but my father would not listen. All his words were of revenge for the harm done to the honour of our family. And for this revenge he goes to Kyrios Andreas, who is a brother to us in all but blood.'

Gemma flushed angrily. 'Why should he do that? I'm surprised your father didn't simply arrange to—pass me round the family.'

Maria looked shocked. 'He could not do such a thing, *thespinis*. It would cause shame to my mother, and to the wives of my brothers. Besides,' she added on a more practical note, 'our house is next to that of the priest. The *papa* would be angry to hear such talk of vengeance. But if he hears that there is a woman here with Kyrios Andreas, he will not think it strange, although he may shake his head,' she added quaintly.

Gemma was thinking rapidly, 'And if he knew the truth, he'd probably blow his top.' She looked appealingly at the other girl. 'Maria I'm not really dressed for visiting, as you can see, but you could ask the priest, secretly, to come here and speak to me. He'd have to help me if he knew what was going on.' She paused. 'Please Maria—if you care anything for Mike—do this for me.'

Maria spread her hands helplessly. 'I cannot, *thespinis*. Only today, the *papa* has gone from the village to visit his own father who is ill. He has driven to Heraklion in Kyrios Andreas' own jeep with him.'

Gemma said hollowly, 'Oh God,' and sat down on the bottom step. She looked up at Maria. 'When is he expected back?'

Maria shrugged. 'In a few days, perhaps, a week. I do not know. But do not agitate yourself, *thespinis*,' she added hearteningly. 'I have heard my mother say that Kyrios Andreas wearies quickly of his women. Perhaps by that time, you will no longer be here.'

Gemma's lips parted to say something blistering, then closed again. There was no point, she thought wearily, in venting her anger and worry on Maria, who probably thought she was making a lot of unnecessary fuss, judging by the aggravating note of reverence which entered her voice each time she mentioned Andreas.

So, he came from a wealthy and important family. Gemma supposed she might have guessed as much, and was forced to admit to herself that it only added to her problems. Presumably, he could be expected to have some kind of influence with the authorities, and she might have trouble getting her story believed.

She remembered bitterly his own cynical remark 'a little adventure with a rich Greek' and realised with something approaching despair that it was a

view it would be only too easy for other people to
share. Certainly, the truth sounded preposterous,
and who would vouch for the fact that she'd been
held at the Villa Ione against her will? Maria?
Never in this world, she told herself realistically.
Maria might not agree with her family's methods
of avenging their honour, but she would never say
so publicly.

She said slowly, 'You asked me where Mike had
gone, Maria. Have you really no idea yourself?
You must have seen him just before he left. Did he
give no hint? Leave no clue?'

Maria looked as if she was going to cry. 'None,
thespinis. All that I know is that he was going to
join a friend of his, nothing more.'

'You never heard him mention this friend's
name?' Gemma demanded. 'Was he another
Englishman.'

Maria shrugged evasively, her full lips pouting a
little. 'I do not think so.'

'A Greek?' Gemma prompted. 'A Cretan,
perhaps?'

Maria walked towards the kitchen with a
flounce of her red skirt. 'I will not answer all these
questions,' she flung back over her shoulder.
'Your brother promised to help me, and now he
has gone, and I do not think he will come back,
because he is frightened. He has broken his
promise to me, so why should I help you—*vromo
anglitha*,' she added venomously.

Gemma felt bewildered by this sudden change in
attitude. She said, 'I'm sorry, Maria, but I'm upset
too. I've been kidnapped, and that's a very serious
offence in my country. This Kyrios Andreas of
yours could be in big trouble . . .'

Maria sneered. 'Trouble? For you, perhaps,
thespinis, but not for Andreas. You say you were

kidnapped—but all the world saw you come here, walking on your own legs up to the villa, *po po po*. Who heard you scream? Who has heard you cry for help? No one, and if questions are asked that is what we shall say. We shall say that you were the *eromeni* of Andreas, and that you followed him here, and that you say terrible things about him because he has tired of you, because he no longer desires a pale skinny English girl in his bed.'

Gemma said acidly, 'Your command of the English language has improved amazingly, Maria. May I ask if you have a reason for being here, or did you just come to look me over?'

'I came for the laundry which my aunt will wash,' Maria said sulkily.

Gemma raised her eyebrows. 'Well at least that's one domestic chore I'm being spared.' She tried not to sound too defeated, but it wasn't easy. Maria had been a doubtful ally from the start, but Gemma had thought she might be prepared to help her in some way, if only for Mike's sake. But the girl was obviously bitter at his desertion, and Gemma supposed she couldn't blame her.

She said, more gently, 'Maria, I'm sure my brother will come back.'

Maria shrugged. 'I no longer care whether he does or not,' she said rudely. 'Now, I take the laundry.'

She took it, wrapped in one of the bed sheets from upstairs. She did not look at Gemma again, or speak, as she walked through the living area, and disappeared with a swing of her hips towards the terrace steps.

Impulsively, Gemma started after her. She couldn't let her go like this—when for a few moments they'd seemed so close to an understanding. Surely she could make Maria see that she wouldn't endear herself to Mike by allowing his only sister to become some stranger's unwilling mistress.

She was at the door, when she heard the dog's warning growl just behind her. She took another step, and felt herself held, the hem of the shirt she was wearing clamped in the animal's jaws. Its eyes gleamed at her malevolently. It was growling in its throat, and she could feel its breath hot on the skin of her thigh.

With a groan, she turned back into the room, and immediately felt herself released.

She said with great distinctness, 'You bloody animal,' and burst into tears.

No day had ever seemed so long.

The hands on her watch seemed to crawl round, each five-minute interval like an hour in duration. She was on edge all the time listening for the sound of the jeep, awaiting—dreading—his return.

At lunchtime, she made a sandwich, using some of the bread from breakfast with the lamb. She ate ravenously, surprised at her own appetite. She had started to believe she would never eat again. In fact, her own hunger made her ashamed, and she was thankful she was alone, and could indulge it unobserved.

She offered the dog some meat, but it refused point blank to take it from her hand. She put the lamb bone down on the floor and presently it carried it into a corner and began to gnaw, but Gemma wasn't fooled into thinking this might represent some kind of truce between them. She'd tried two more casual strolls towards the terrace steps, each time with the same result.

The dog had been polite but firm, she thought with irony. However, she was under no illusion that the politeness would necessarily continue if she persisted.

During the long afternoon, she remembered the paperback novel she'd taken to the sun terrace the previous day, and retrieved it, but it was no real help. The trials of the heroine seemed to pale into insignificance when compared to her own.

She debated about sunbathing; wondered what Andreas would do if she allowed herself to be burned raw; decided the attendant risks were too great, and sneered at herself for being a coward.

There was sun filter cream in her toilet bag. She used it, and for the first time in her life sunbathed nude, turning herself delicately and languorously in the hot rays, enjoying the sensation of freedom it gave her. This time, however, she was careful not to fall asleep.

The sun was already sinking down behind the mountain peaks when she went for her shower. Andreas—her mind used his name tentatively, more accustomed to thinking of him as the Cretan, or, more simply even, the stranger—had still not returned. Not that she wanted him to, she thought stormily. In fact, it would give her infinite satisfaction to know that he and his damned jeep were at the bottom of some precipice, with the buzzards already circling overhead. But his return would mean she'd have some decent clothes to wear again. Being only half-dressed like this made her vulnerable, undermined her morale, she thought, and it was no earthly use reminding herself that during the ordinary course of her holiday only a short while before she'd worn scarcely any more. That was different, and she knew it. And, presumably, he knew it too.

He'd worked out his plan of campaign very carefully, Gemma thought savagely. He knew exactly how to play upon her hopes, her fears, and, she had to admit, her desires.

She shivered as she stepped under the jets of the shower, but not simply because of the impact of the cool droplets on her heated skin. Oh God, but he was dangerous, and she'd known it from the first moment she saw him. Dark as the devil, arrogant as one of the gods of old in this land, powerful as the Lord of Life and Death who'd ruled in his bull mask at Knossos, taking tribute from the alien captives brought in chains across the sea.

Closing her eyes, she lifted her face to the cascading water, letting it pour through her hair and over her shoulders. Then with a little sigh of satisfaction, she turned off the flow.

There was no warning—none at all. The dog hadn't uttered, and the noise of the shower had effectually blocked out all other sounds.

She turned, reaching for a towel, and saw him standing in the doorway, watching her. He was smiling faintly as the dark eyes coolly assessed every inch of her naked body.

Her first instinct was to shrink, to cover herself somehow with her hands, her hair, yet something told her that such a belated and useless attempt at modesty would only amuse him further. It would be just another petty victory for him if she seemed to care too much about herself so completely. Far better to brazen it out, to let him think his presence here was immaterial because she despised him. Her eyes flared contempt at him, and her chin lifted defiantly as she scooped the heavy strands of damp blonde back from her face, and tossed them over her shoulders. The gesture arched her small high breasts, a fact he acknowledged with a mocking downward slant of his mouth.

Then he moved, stepping towards her, his purpose clear in the sudden intensity of his dark gaze, and Gemma moved too, at speed, all her bravado disintegrating as she grabbed frantically for the errant towel. Her foot slipped on the damp tiles, and she fell down on one knee, cracking the bone painfully as she did so. She cried out involuntarily and at once he was beside her, his hands under her shoulders lifting her effortlessly.

'You are hurt? Tell me . . .'

He carried her into the adjoining bedroom and put her down on the bed. The discarded shirt was lying there and she seized it and held it in front of her.

'Don't touch me.' Bright spots of colour burned in her face. 'Get out of my room.'

He'd been bending over her, but at her words, he straightened and stood back, the concern in his face giving way to overt amusement.

He pointed to the shirt. 'Isn't that a little late?' he asked, laughing.

That this was her own view as well made it no easier to bear. She glared at him savagely. 'Kidnapper, rapist and now Peeping Tom,' she hurled at him recklessly. 'What a full life you lead, *kyrie*, or should I say—Andreas.'

There was a brief electric pause. His mouth twisted. 'So—you have had a visitor. Once more, it seems, Maria's curiosity has outrun her discretion.'

'Oh, you mustn't blame her for telling me. She must have thought that, as your mistress, I would at least know your Christian name if nothing else about you.'

'It is not her place to think about such matters at all,' he said icily. 'What else did you discuss?'

She shrugged. 'Very little. Religion—briefly—

and the fact that she's no longer in love with Mike.'

'Did you think she ever was? You are a romantic, Gemma *mou*. Love does not describe the kind of brief, sordid association she and your brother shared. If they had—loved, he would have courted her with honour—asked her to be his wife.'

It was odd how those contemptuous words hurt her, more even than the pain in her bruised knee.

She said stonily, 'Then it's fortunate for them both that you've avenged the family honour and saved them the necessity of being miserable together. And now perhaps you'd let me have some privacy, because I'd like to get dressed.' She took a breath. 'I assume you've brought me some clothes.'

'I have warned you before about making assumptions, Gemma.' His tone was sardonic. 'By day, you are already adequately covered by what you can filch from my wardrobe. If you feel you need an alternative for the rest of the time—I have brought you one.'

He reached into his pocket, and produced a square packet which he tossed to her. She caught it awkwardly, one-handed, still clinging to the shirt with the other. A bikini, she wondered, or underwear. But, no. The parcel was too small, surely, and too heavy as well. She eased the outer wrapping with her thumbnail, and took off the paper. The decorated box inside was familiar. She looked down at the lettering almost stupidly. '*Shalimar*? But that's . . .'

'The perfume you brought from England,' he completed the thought for her.' It is a favourite of mine too. How nice, *matia mou*, that our tastes are the same.'

'Nice?' Gemma repeated dazedly. 'Nice? My God.' She jumped to her feet, regardless of her throbbing knee. 'How dare you do this? Haven't you degraded me enough already?'

'You find French perfume degrading?' His brows lifted. 'You must be unique.'

'It isn't the bloody scent.' Her voice throbbed with temper. 'It's the—the implication, and you know it. As an alternative to your loathsome shirts, I'm to wear this—and nothing else, I suppose. Your own private strip show. Well, I'll see you in hell first. If you like it so much, wear it yourself.' She threw the bottle at him, but he caught it adroitly before it smashed, to her chagrin. 'Or better still, keep it for your next lady. She may share your—your perverted appetites. I don't.'

'As you wish.' He put the box back in his pocket. His face and voice were expressionless, but she knew that he was angry just the same. He said, too gently, 'My appetites are quite normal, I believe. As for your own, my lovely one, I suspect that in spite of your protestations, they are still unawakened.' He paused. 'A situation,' he added with cool deliberation, 'that I intend to remedy later.'

He went out, closing the door behind him.

CHAPTER SIX

THE light faded out of the sky, and she watched it go with a kind of quiet desperation. The arrival of darkness seemed an omen of all her worst nightmares, and she was scared.

As soon as she was alone, she'd dressed hurriedly, fastening all the buttons on the shirt from throat to hem with finicking and ridiculous care, and winding the sash tightly round her slim waist. As if it would really make the slightest difference in the end, she thought despairingly.

Then she'd sat on the edge of the bed, one palm cupped round her sore knee and waited.

She could hear the sound of the shower from his room, and the silence when it ceased. Later, she'd heard the door of his room open, and his footsteps and in spite of herself, she'd shrunk back on the bed, staring at the door, anticipating its opening. But he'd walked past, without even the slightest hesitation, and gone downstairs.

That had been nearly twenty minutes ago, and now the delicious aroma of grilling meat was floating up to her, reminding her with potent cruelty just how long ago it was since she'd eaten that sandwich.

Gemma licked her lips. There was little point in remaining where she was, cowering in a corner until he chose to come for her, especially when she had no means of keeping him away. She'd even tried to shift the chest of drawers to block the door, but it had been too heavy for her, and she hadn't been able to budge it by as much as an inch.

All she could do was go downstairs and hope somehow to find a way to persuade him to give her some further respite. She bit her lip nervously. Probably it hadn't been very wise to make him angry, to have thrown an expensive gift literally back in his face, but she couldn't honestly say she regretted it, she thought fiercely, her hands curling into claws. And anyway, it was safer to be on hostile terms with him. She could fight his anger with her own. It was when his voice gentled—when he came close to her—touched her—that he was most dangerous.

She shuddered, remembering the moment when he'd picked her up from the bathroom floor, his hands momentarily grazing her breasts as he did so. He hadn't even intended a caress, yet the shock of it had shaken her as if the earth had moved under her feet.

If she kept him angry, perhaps she could also keep him at arm's length, she thought.

The door to his room was ajar, and he'd left the lamp burning on the chest of drawers. Gemma paused, wondering whether she should extinguish it, and then she saw the bunch of keys lying next to it. Car keys, she thought incredulously. The keys to the jeep, there for the taking. She was already stretching out her hand, when she remembered she had no pockets to hide them in. Besides, if she took them now, and hid them in her own room, he might miss them. Whereas, if she left them where they were for the time being, and took them while he was asleep as she'd planned originally, then the first he'd know about it was when he awoke the next day, and found her gone and the jeep too.

But she was sorely tempted to grab the whole bunch and make a dash for it here and now. The main problem was still Cerberus. She hadn't heard a yelp out of him since Andreas had returned, but that didn't mean he wasn't lurking about downstairs, just waiting for her to make one false move.

And when she got downstairs, and realised that Andreas himself was on the terrace, cooking steaks on a charcoal grill, she was more than ever thankful that she'd decided to wait.

He had his back turned to her, seemingly intent on his task, but as she got to the doorway, he said coolly, *'Kalispera.'*

Gemma swallowed. 'Good evening,' she returned with an assumption of calmness.

'The food is nearly ready.' He gestured towards the table where a salad and a bottle of red wine were already waiting.

'So I see.' She paused. 'I gather I've been demoted from chef.'

He gave her an enigmatic look. 'Some of your recipes are a little too ingenious, *matia mou*. Who knows? You might have gone wandering in the hills today and found some hemlock.'

'With the Hound of the Baskervilles to keep me company?' she asked sweetly. 'Even I'm not that ingenious, *kyrie*. And where is Cerberus, by the way?'

'He has gone back to his master,' he said, 'who lives in the village, not the Underworld. You miss the dog perhaps? You would like to have him as a pet while you are here?'

'I can think of only a few things I would like less,' Gemma said, still sweetly.

'And I'm sure I don't even have to ask what they are.' He transferred the steaks deftly to plates and handed her one. 'I hope you don't intend to refuse this too.'

She would have loved to have had the moral strength to fling the steak off the terrace into the bushes, but she was so hungry she could have eaten the plate as well, so she merely smiled noncommittally as she watched him pour wine into her glass.

'You don't have a dog of your own?'

He shook his head. 'I am here so little, it would not be fair.'

'But then what is?' Gemma said blandly. 'I've seen a cat.'

'Did you feed it?'

She hesitated. 'Not really. I put down a few scraps this morning.'

'Then I am only surprised you have not seen a hundred cats,' he said. 'They are not the sleek pampered pets you have in England. Here, they breed, and they beg.' He gave her a sardonic smile. 'And now we have finished with the animal kingdom, Gemma *mou*, what safe topic do you suggest for discussion next?'

She shrugged. 'As far as I'm concerned, we don't have to talk at all.' She cut into her steak as if it were someone's throat.

'You have a gift for silence?' His brows lifted. 'An amazing quality in a woman.'

'My speciality.' She sipped her wine. 'As chauvinist remarks seem to be yours.'

'I specialise in other things as well,' he said gently.

She glared at him mutely over the rim of her wine glass. There was a long pause, then Gemma said abruptly, 'Did Michael have a special friend in the village? A man friend, I mean.'

'Not that I am aware of. He knew Stavros, of course, and Maria's brothers.' He took more salad. 'You have some reason for asking?'

'Not really.' She speared a piece of tomato. 'It was just something Maria said to me. She told me Mike had gone to meet a friend, and I got the impression this friend could be Greek.'

'It would be no one from this village.' He frowned a little. 'He no longer has friends here. But I believe he stayed in other places before he came to Loussenas.'

She sighed. 'I suppose he must have done.' And she had little chance of tracing any of these places, she thought despondently. Crete was a big island, and although she thought Mike in one of his infrequent letters had mentioned some place in the White Mountains, she couldn't be sure.

She said, 'I wouldn't be too sure that it's no one from this village. Perhaps not everyone thinks Maria's the wronged maiden her family like to make out. I think she knows this friend of Michael's because she got very angry when I pressed the point.'

'Perhaps Maria does not think it necessary to keep her temper with the sister of her seducer,' he said grimly. 'Anyway, she had no right to be here. I shall speak to Stavros tomorrow.'

Go and speak to him now, Gemma prompted silently, and the last you'll see of me will be the jeep's tail lights disappearing down the mountainside.

But, of course, he did nothing of the sort. When she had finished her steak, he asked if she would like some fruit. She was on the point of refusing when she remembered that even if she was no longer hungry, fruit would be a way of prolonging the meal. But when he made to refill her glass, she hastily put her hand over it. It was heady stuff, she'd discovered already, and she needed to keep her wits about her.

He cleared the plates and came back with a bowl of fruit, and two small cups of coffee, thick and rather bitter.

She said, 'Is this what we call Turkish coffee?'

'You may, Gemma *mou*, but we do not. Relations between our countries have been strained and worse for generations.'

'It's sad,' she said, half to herself. 'Turkey's such a near neighbour to Greece to be an enemy.'

'Everywhere in the world there are such problems.' He shrugged slightly. 'In the case of your own country, there is Ireland, I think.'

She took some grapes from the bowl, and began to eat them. They were the size of small plums, purple and thick with juice. There was silence between them, but the night was full of sounds— the chirping of cicadas in the undergrowth, the cry of a bird, far off, mournful and piercing, and closer at hand, music.

Gemma pushed back her chair, and went over to the balustrade. 'What's that?'

There was a moon, she noticed, a great golden ball swinging in the heavens on a chain of stars.

She heard him get up too. Was suddenly aware he was standing behind her, very close to her.

He said, 'The music? They are having a celebration in the village.'

'Don't tell me.' She kept her tone light, but she was acutely conscious of him, of his breath stirring her hair, the warmth of his body subtly penetrating her thin layer of clothing. 'They're having a public stoning.'

'They are good people,' he said quietly. 'Under other circumstances, Gemma *mou*, you would think so too.'

His hand closed on her hip, swaying her backwards so that she was actually leaning against him. She felt his lips touch her ear, his teeth gently grazing the lobe, and she tensed. His mouth moved downwards, teasing a sensitive path down to the curve of her shoulder. The music in the distance was playing an insistent, insidious rhythm, and her pulses echoed it, while the moonlight swam behind her closed lids.

His other hand cupped her breast, caressing its rounded softness, before his fingers sought the hardening thrust of her nipple through the fabric of the shirt. The barrier of the material between his seeking and her urgency was a delicately erotic torment. She was suddenly scorched by the memory of his hands brushing against her bare breasts, and the knowledge of how desperately she needed to feel his hands on her body again shook her to the soul.

If she moved, even slightly, turned fully into his arms, offered him her mouth, then there would be no going back—and no escape either.

She whispered, 'No' frantically, and pulled away from him. She'd made her plans and no shock of desire, no fever of the blood, was going to stop her now. But was the choice even hers anymore, she wondered as his hands came down on her shoulders, turning her to face him.

His voice was deep, urgent. It made her shiver. 'Forget, *matia mou*. Forget everything except that we are here together and we want each other.'

'I can't,' she said hoarsely. 'I can't forget. You—you must give me more time—please. If you'll wait, I'll do anything you want, be anything you want—I swear it. Only not now, not yet, I beg you.'

She swallowed, waiting in a kind of agony for his reply.

She heard him murmur something which could

have been an obscenity or a prayer, then his hand took her chin, turning her face up to his.

'What are you trying to do to me, Gemma?' he asked huskily. 'Is this how you've treated your other men—putting them into hell while you offer them heaven?'

She shook her head, avoiding the intensity of his dark eyes. 'That—that was a lie. There's never been ... I've never ...' She stumbled to a halt. 'Oh, I don't expect you to believe me.'

'No, I think that is the truth—at last,' he said grimly. 'Does it also explain your reluctance, I wonder?' He shook his head slowly. 'That—I cannot believe. You are not a child, but a beautiful woman.'

She flicked the tip of her tongue along her dry lips. 'You said you'd be patient,' she reminded him.

He smiled wryly. 'And you catch me in my own trap, Gemma *mou*. If you remember too, I said my patience was not endless.'

She stared, as if mesmerised, at the open neck of his shirt and the black hair which shadowed the golden skin it revealed. 'I remember.' Her voice shook a little. 'But it won't be for much longer.'

'Is that a promise?' He was frowning slightly.

'A promise.'

'Then we have a bargain.' He paused. 'You are a creature of moods, Gemma. One moment a virago, screaming abuse at me—the next, a cooing dove. Which, I wonder, is nearest the truth—nearest the woman who lives behind your eyes?' He brushed a gentle finger across her lids. 'The woman who wishes to spend yet another night alone.'

He released her, and she stepped back, trying to

stem the flood of relief rising inside her in case it
showed, and made him suspicious. But he turned
away, pouring himself more wine, and she seized
the opportunity to slip away. She washed the
dishes and put them away, then went up to her
room. She glanced into his room, and saw the keys
still there on the chest. She gave them a longing
glance, and hoped Andreas wasn't planning on
spending half the night on the terrace drinking
wine and listening to the music.

She didn't undress, but slipped as she was under
the covering sheet. She was nervous and excited,
but made herself relax, because she might have to
wait quite a while. In the end, she dozed a little,
and eventually woke with a start, convinced it was
morning and her chance to escape missed
completely.

But the room was still bright with moonlight,
and the house was filled with a deep quietness.

She slid out of bed and padded to the door,
opening it cautiously and listening. Still no sound.

She crept back into the bathroom and collected
her toilet bag. It was all she possessed in the world,
and she had no intention of leaving it behind,
although it seemed she was forced to abandon the
rest of her belongings for the time being. Including
her passport and her travellers cheques, she
thought, biting her lip. But she'd be back for them,
bringing the authorities with her.

She tiptoed across the passage. His door was
closed, but the handle turned easily and quietly
under her fingers, and she slid into the room like a
little ghost.

All she had to do was pick up the keys and go,
but something impelled her to take one last look at
him. He was asleep, half-turned on to his side, his
skin very dark against the stark whiteness of the

bedlinen. The rumpled sheet draped across his hips in no way disguised the fact that he was naked.

He looked younger, she thought with an odd little catch of the breath, with some of that proud arrogance muted by slumber.

For a long moment, she stood, staring down at him, her mind playing tricks, her imagination taking her down paths she had never before wanted to tread. Then, her lower lip caught in her teeth to bite back what might have been a sigh, she tiptoed to the chest and picked up the keys with infinite care.

She seemed to be saying goodbye with every step of the stairs as she descended. Her captivity had lasted hours rather than days, but already in some strange way the house seemed as familiar to her as—as her own home in England. She gave herself an angry mental shake. She should be thanking her stars she was escaping, relatively unscathed, not indulging in stupid and unnecessary nostalgia.

The jeep was parked off the track just under the wall. She approached it with a certain amount of trepidation. But—she could drive, therefore it followed that she could drive this, and the fact that her licence was in England, and she was not insured were details she hoped she would never have to discuss with anyone.

She slid in behind the wheel, and felt for the ignition. She tried each key in turn, and because it was dark and she was nervous, she missed the right one, and had to start again. This time, she counted them off in her head as she used them. And again, by some mischance, she missed.

Get a grip, she adjured herself silently, taking a deep breath. Third time has to be lucky.

He said, 'Those are the keys to my sports car, Gemma. Do you think I am quite a fool?'

She almost screamed, and the keys fell clattering to the floor of the jeep. She bent to retrieve them, but he was there before her, picking them up with one hand, clasping her wrist with the other.

His voice went on mockingly, 'You were almost convincing, my cooing dove, with your virginal fears. But at the same time, I was sure you could not resist the bait, if it was offered.' Insolently he dangled the keys in front of her. 'And I was right.'

Her voice shook. 'Damn you to hell.'

He grinned. 'The return of the virago. I am not sure I do not welcome it. I wonder how many other facets of your personality I shall discover before the night is over?' His grip tightened on her wrist. 'Now come with me.'

She had no choice. She realised now there had never really been one. She had been playing a game, but he'd been dictating the rules, every step of the way. And, when he wished, changing them.

In the living room, he had lit a lamp. He had dragged on a pair of jeans, but he was barefoot, bare-chested, and she looked at the lithe body which would soon possess her own, and knew that he had the power to possess her soul too. And she knew she could not let that happen. She remembered Maria's words, '*Andreas wearies quickly of his women*' with a pang. That was what she had to guard against—the moment when he sent her away, because he had no further use for her as an instrument of vengeance, or more damagingly, as a woman.

He said, 'You are shivering, *matia mou*.' He held out a hand to her. The gesture and the smile which went with it teased and beckoned. 'Let me warm you.'

She took a quick breath. 'No.' She turned away, turning her back quite deliberately on the outstretched hand, and the lure it offered of warmth, of laughter, of passion—and, ultimately, of a heartbreak which could destroy her.

He sighed sharply. 'Gemma, don't be a fool. You knew from the first . . .'

'Yes,' she said. 'You made the position perfectly clear. I know why I'm here, and I know what you intend to do.'

The smile was back in his voice. 'My sweet one, I intend to make love to you.'

She shook her head, staring blindly at the wall. 'No—not love. Earlier today, you spelled out exactly what it would be—"a brief sordid association". Those were your words.'

'Yes.' His tone roughened. 'But I spoke of Maria and your brother, not of ourselves. You misunderstood . . .'

'I've never misunderstood.' Her throat felt tight. 'I know why I'm here, in this situation. And I know that you'll never let me go until I've paid this—this unspeakable debt for Michael. So I will—pay. I accept that's the way it has to be.' She took another long breath. 'And I won't fight. I—I won't try and stop you. You can have me. But that's all you'll have.' She bent her head and stared down at the floor. 'So—so don't try and dress it up with talk of making love, or—or wanting because that's not part of it.'

'You think I don't want you?' There was an odd note in his voice.

'I don't think about it at all, because I don't care.' Her throat felt constricted. 'If going to bed with you is my passport out of here, then I'll go. But—please—no more cat-and-mouse games, and no more talk about making love. Just—do what you want and get it over with.'

There was a long and terrible silence, then he said very quietly, 'You do not know what you are saying.'

She nodded. 'But I do. There's no way you can make this easy for me, so I'd be grateful if you could at least be quick. If you wouldn't mind,' she added, like a polite child.

'But I do mind.' His voice was like molten steel. 'And you will mind too, Gemma. You are not made of wood, so why pretend that you have no feelings?'

'Because it's better to have none,' she said. 'If I allowed myself to feel something, it would be hate—hate for you for bringing me here, hate for myself, for being a woman.' She shook her head. 'I don't want to feel those things—they're damaging, destructive.'

'And indifference is not?' he challenged.

She said wearily, 'I don't know. But it's all I have.'

There was another silence, then he said with cold courtesy, 'Then let it be as you wish.'

They went to his room. She watched him straighten the bed, shake up the pillows, then turned away hastily as he began to unzip his jeans. If she'd secretly hoped that her defiant speech would kill any desire he had for her stone-dead, then she'd miscalculated, she thought wearily.

He said, 'I am waiting.'

She risked a quick glance. He was in bed, propped on one elbow, watching her, his eyes as black as onyx, and as hard.

Gemma cleared her throat. 'Would you put out the lamp please?'

'No.'

As she unwound the sash, she tried to comfort herself with the reminder that he'd seen her in the shower only that afternoon. That, outwardly at least, her body no longer held any secrets for him. But it did not prevent her from fumbling every button.

The walk across the room to the bed seemed the longest she had ever taken. She slid under the sheet and lay next to him, not touching. Her pulses sounded like thunder in her ears. She wondered if he could hear them too.

He put out a hand, and gently stroked a tress of hair back from her forehead.

He said, 'My Gemma, it does not have to be like this between us, and you know it. Turn to me, sweet one. I promise I will make you happy.'

And afterwards unhappy, she thought. When it's over.

She didn't look at him. 'No—this is how it must be.'

He said harshly, 'So be it then. Am I permitted to kiss you—caress you—or would that simply prolong your agony?' He paused, and when she didn't reply gave a short laugh. 'I see. Then, if nothing else, my dove, relax for me, otherwise you will feel pain.'

She felt pain already. It filled her heart and mind. It swamped the universe, but she welcomed it because it helped her to remain detached as his hand swept a slow, remorseless path down her body.

She had said she wouldn't resist, and when the long fingers stroked her thighs, she allowed him to part them, without demur. And he was keeping his side of their cold bargain too, she realised, dazedly accepting his almost clinical exploration of her most intimate self. Whatever she'd been expecting, it had not been this, she thought, trying not to flinch and failing.

He saw, of course. 'I am hurting you?'

Gemma bit her lip. 'You're very—thorough.'

He said coolly, 'And you are very inexperienced. In that, at least, you told the truth.'

She turned her head away and stared at the small flame flickering in the lamp. There was another small flame, somewhere deep inside her, barely alight, struggling for life, which she had to ignore. Because even this bleak, impersonal discovering of her was having its effect on her body's reflexes.

It would be so easy, she thought wretchedly, to reach up and draw him down to her, to put her lips against his face, his skin. So easy, and so fatal.

She stole a glance at him through her lashes. He looked stern—remote, and when he moved over her, she was frightened again, because he was a stranger whom she had absolved of all necessity to be kind. And if he was brutal, she would only have herself to blame, she thought, her nails scoring tense crescents in the palms of her hands.

But when he'd said he could be patient, he had not lied, she discovered wonderingly. She might not have deserved consideration but it was there for her just the same. And skill. And an infinite control which reduced the initial pain of his possession that her taut, unyielding muscles had made inevitable.

And, as he entered her completely, she cried out, not just because of the hurting, but in amazement too that this joining of their bodies which should have been so traumatic was, in the end, so incredibly, miraculously simple.

He took a corner of the sheet, and gently wiped the tiny beads of sweat from her forehead and cheekbones, and in that moment she let herself acknowledge freely for the first time that she loved him. That the ultimate disaster which she had tried to avoid had already overtaken her.

And she acknowledged too, as he began to move inside her slowly at first, that this brief treasuring of his warmth and strength as part of her would be all of him she would ever have to remember.

Echoing his own words, she thought, 'So be it, then.'

As he reached his climax he groaned something—her name—some words in his own language, then rolled away from her burying his face in the pillow, while his harsh, ragged breathing slowly steadied.

Gemma lay beside him, not speaking, aching, wondering what she should do next. Go back to her own room, perhaps?

After a while, he flung back the sheet and got out of bed, crossing the room to the bathroom.

She heard the sound of running water. Perhaps this was a signal for her to take her leave she thought, lifting herself up, and wincing a little. But the next minute he was back, carrying a bowl of water and a small towel. He sat on the edge of the bed, and began to bathe her with the dampened towel, first her face, and then, drawing back the sheet, her body.

She saw without surprise that she had bled a little. It was strange, she thought, but oddly sweet to lie there, allowing him to perform this intimate, but at the same time impersonal service for her.

When he had finished, he put the bowl down beside the bed, and let the towel drop to the floor beside it.

She said quietly, 'May I go now?'

'No,' he said. 'You may not.' There was a note

in his voice which seemed to warn her not to press the point.

He lay down beside her again, pulling the sheet to cover them both, and blew out the lamp. His arm went round her shoulders, pulling her down to him, pillowing her head on his chest. His other hand closed round the curve of her hip, drawing her closer to the warmth of his naked body. Cradled against him, she felt the tensions and the misery slowly begin to ebb away. His skin felt like silk under her cheek, the beat of his heart like the pulse of the universe under her hand.

After what had happened, it was madness, she thought, to feel so safe, so comforted.

Yet, after a while, against the odds, against all reason, she fell asleep in his arms.

CHAPTER SEVEN

SHE awoke to the beauty of a dawn sky and the realisation that she was being watched. She turned her head a fraction and looked into his eyes.

He brushed his mouth lightly across hers, and she knew what had woken her.

'You have rested well?' he asked.

Her, 'Yes' sounded strangled, because the hand that had been resting on her hip travelled upwards, and was now cupping her pointed breast, his thumb lazily stroking her nipple, sending fierce shafts of pleasure through her.

'And I did not hurt you too much?' He bent his head, and trailed a pattern of tiny kisses around the breast he was caressing, taking the aroused rosy peak between his lips, and tugging it sensuously.

She gasped. 'What are you doing?'

He lifted his head and smiled at her. 'Making love to you, *agape mou*, as I should have done last night.' He kissed her other breast, his tongue moving against her skin, filling her with piercing excitement.

She said hoarsely, 'No.'

'Yes,' he contradicted her, a sudden fierceness in his eyes and voice. 'Last night, Gemma, you made me feel like an animal. You will not do so twice. From this moment, I want to feel human again, to feel as a man should do with his woman.'

'I'm not your woman.' It was the only defence she could think of, and a poor one as it turned out, because he only grinned at her sardonically, and flung the sheet which was her only protection off the bed.

'Tell me that later,' he invited. 'Much later,' he added huskily, and kissed her indignantly parted lips very slowly and very completely. When at last he raised his head, she couldn't think of a single thing to say. She lay back against his encircling arm and looked up at him, her eyes widening endlessly. Every nerve in her body seemed tinglingly awake, the blood moving slowly through her veins, as thick and sweet as honey. She was aware of that deep inner trembling, and knew now that it was desire, that her body was crying out for the fulfilment it had been denied.

He kissed her mouth again, her eyes, the swift unsteady pulse in her throat. She wondered helplessly how she could ever have thought his mouth hard, when it was like velvet against her skin, his tongue a sweet flame, setting her alight in turn . . .

His fingers caressed her, moulding every curve and plane of her slender body, and where his hand touched, his lips followed in an erotic pilgrimage which made her moan aloud, half in protest, half in yearning.

She moved against him restlessly, driven by instincts she still barely understood, kissing his shoulder, her small teeth grazing the smooth skin. She wanted to please him in turn, to create the same kind of delight for him, but she didn't know how, and then he took her hands and guided them to his body, and showed her.

She'd always considered herself a girl of her times, informed and intelligent about sex, knowledgeable about the physiology of her own body. But now she knew how wide a gulf there was between theory and practice. No book, no lesson, had ever taught her that one man's hands caressing her breasts, one man's mouth unhurriedly exploring the hollow inside her hip bone could turn her responses to frenzy. Nothing had warned her of the pleasure, even pride, to be gained from feeling his own body quicken in answer to her first shy, unpractised advances.

She heard him groan her name, his face taut, almost fierce, then he was above her and within her, and they were one, driven and consumed by the same passionate, primitive hunger.

There was sunlight in the room, touching him like an aureole, turning his lean body to gold, and it was part of her too, she discovered—a great sunburst of sensation, exploding in the deepest core of her being, and rippling through every fibre of her in spasm after spasm of uncontrollable pleasure.

She cried his name, the sound torn out of her in a kind of agony, and heard him answer, then his mouth took hers in an endless kiss as the storm of feeling slowly subsided, and they slid, still locked together, into calmer waters.

A long time later, he said, 'Talk to me.'

'About what?' She still felt almost dazed, her body weightless with contentment. If his arm had not been across her, anchoring her, she would have floated, she thought idly.

'About yourself. This career you once spoke of, for example.'

'You won't find it very interesting,' she said. 'I demonstrate and sell electronic typewriters, and word processing equipment.'

'For yourself?'

'Heavens, no, for a company—Protechnics Limited. Graham employs a team of girls.'

'This Graham is your boss? Tell me about him.'

She tried to think what there was to say about Graham. Not that it was easy to think of anything except that Andreas' hand was stroking her arm very gently, tracing with one forefinger the delicate tracery of veins inside her elbow.

She said, 'Well—he's kind and practical, and a very shrewd businessman, although he's always moaning that the company's on the edge of disaster. We all like him.'

'Is he young?' He picked up her hand and carried it to his lips, kissing each finger in turn. 'Middle-aged? Married?'

She laughed a little breathlessly. 'He's nearly forty, and very much married, with three children. His wife works for the company too.'

'This is usual in your country for a wife to identify herself so closely with her husband's business?' His mouth caressed the softness of her palm.

'I'd say that would depend very much on the business.' It was getting increasingly harder to string coherent words together.

'Perhaps. And the children—you said three— what happens to them?'

'They're all at school. And Jennifer has an *au pair*.' She stole a look at him under her lashes, noting a slight tightening of his mouth. 'You obviously don't approve.'

He shrugged. 'How other men live their lives is hardly my concern. But remembering the needs of my own childhood, I am glad that my mother was always there. No nursemaid, however kind, could ever have taken her place.'

'Is—is your mother still alive?'

'Very much alive.'

'And were you an only child?'

'By no means.' He kissed the inside of her wrist very softly, making her pulses leap frantically. 'I have a brother and two sisters, all younger than myself.'

'So you're the head of the family.' Her voice almost cracked in her effort to keep it under control.

'Yes.' It was as if a door had suddenly closed. He kissed her hand again, and rolled away on to his back, staring up at the ceiling.

It was absurd to feel so bereft, she thought faintly. Absurd, and shaming too.

Downstairs, she was suddenly aware of faint sounds of movement. He slanted a look at her. 'Our breakfast has arrived,' he said lightly. 'Are you hungry?'

Her mouth felt dry. 'A little.'

'Then I'll fetch us some food.' He yawned slightly, and stretched, his body lithe and bronzed in the sunshine, making her stingingly aware of the superb play of muscle and sinew. He turned his head and looked at her. Looking at him. She glanced away but not quickly enough, it seemed. Because he said softly, 'Unless you have other plans?'

'No,' she denied hastily. 'None at all.'

He smiled at her lazily. 'Then let me teach you some Greek.' He paused. 'Say after me, *"Mine etho mazi mou"*.' He said the words again slowly, making her repeat them after him. 'Very good, *agape mou*. Now say, *"Se thelo poli"*.'

She complied, looking at him suspiciously. 'I already have a phrasebook. What am I saying?'

His smile widened wickedly. 'What you were too shy to say in your own tongue, my Gemma. You told me "Stay here with me. I want you very much".'

She gasped, 'Oh,' her cheeks burning. 'Oh—you're a bastard. And it isn't true.'

'Is it not?' The long arms captured her effortlessly, pulling her to him. He whispered against her lips. 'Then prove it . . .'

Gemma stepped out from the shower, and wound a towel round her body before going back into the bedroom. Andreas had opened the windows fully before going downstairs, and the sun was streaming in. She stepped out on to the little balcony, and stood drying her hair with her fingers.

She ached, but not unpleasantly, and at the same time she felt vividly, shiningly alive. The air had never seemed so clear, the colours of the rock, the sky, the foliage so sharp and new.

Glancing at herself in the mirror, she had almost been surprised to see she looked the same as usual. Well almost the same, she thought smiling a little. Her mouth looked slightly swollen, and there were faint marks on her shoulders and breasts and thighs which had never been there before.

Their last coming together might have started out in laughter, but it had ended in an almost savage urgency, her body matching his in the fierceness of its demands. When it was over, she had cried, and he had held her closely, comforting her as if she was a child.

She flexed her shoulders in the sun's warmth, narrowing her eyes against the glare. Only she wasn't a child any more. She was a woman, with all a woman's certainties, a woman's power. His woman.

Out of the corner of her eye, she saw a movement, a splash of colour which had not been there before, and she turned her head sharply, her attention focused.

It was Maria, her red dress sharply contrasting with the white dazzle of the rock she was silhouetted against as she climbed the track up the mountain.

Gemma frowned. It was obvious the Greek girl didn't want to be seen, by the way she kept glancing back over her shoulder towards the village path. At first, Gemma wondered whether she could be running away, but she seemed to have nothing with her in the way of luggage. And if she was simply on her way to visit another village, why was she behaving so furtively?

But Gemma thought, with a mental shrug, it was no concern of hers what Maria might be up to. And then stopped dead, her mind almost blanking out with shock. Because she'd almost— almost forgotten in the dazed aftermath of her first experience of passion, why exactly she was at the villa.

If it had not been for Maria she would have come to Crete, met Michael somewhere and possibly spent a few days sightseeing in his company. Because of Maria, Andreas had come into her life, not as her lover, but as an avenger, and now she had to face the bitter acknowledgment that their hours together in that bed had been primarily the exactment of that vengeance.

She shivered, as if a cloud had passed over the sun. He'd done exactly as he'd threatened he would do—taken her for his pleasure, without love or the promise of commitment, and now she was left with the shame of that knowledge.

It seemed ironic that only a few days before, she'd been complaining to Hilary how all the men she met seemed to want to rush into serious relationships.

I like to take things slowly, she reminded herself painfully, one step at a time. And yet here I am— over my head, and out of my depth.

And she couldn't even pretend she hadn't seen the danger, because she'd recognised it from the first moment she saw him.

She bent her head, and a sigh shook her whole body. Last night, she'd known exactly what she was doing. She'd fought her senses with her mind, and won a small, bitter victory. She should have gone on fighting, but she'd been betrayed by her love for him, and by the needs she hadn't even known existed in her.

But he'd known, she thought wretchedly. He was diabolically experienced. Every time he'd touched her, kissed her, he'd been gauging the sleeping sensuality within her, and planning how to awaken it.

At dawn, that was how, she thought stormily, when she was half-asleep and vulnerable, and bewildered by the gentleness he'd shown her. And she'd forgotten everything—everything except how much she wanted him.

She only hoped she would be able to forget everything that had happened between them as easily.

She started violently as his hands descended on her shoulders.

'What are you dreaming of?' His mouth brushed the side of her throat.

She said woodenly, 'I was just looking at the view.' She pointed. 'What's up that track?'

He shrugged. 'Very little. A few goats, many stones, and an old hut which the shepherds use. Why do you ask?'

'I thought there might be another village.' She turned back into the bedroom.

'Still trying to run away, Gemma *mou*?' He spoke lightly, but his eyes were narrowed.

'No.' She shook her head. 'As you mentioned, dressed like this I wouldn't get very far.'

'But with your clothes, and in the jeep, you could get as far as Aghios Nikolaos.'

Her heart seemed to miss a beat. 'You—you're letting me go?'

'No, little fool.' He dropped a kiss on her bare shoulder. 'I have to go there on business later, and I thought you might like to go with me.' He paused. 'Well? What do you say?'

She shrugged pettishly, moving away from him. 'What's the alternative. Another day alone with Cerberus?'

'Perhaps.'

'Then I'll go to Aghios Nikolaos,' she said ungraciously, and he laughed.

'You are indeed a woman of contrasts, *agape mou*. In bed, a passionate angel. At breakfast, a grudging shrew. I suppose I must thank God it is not the other way about.' He indicated the tray he had placed on the bed. 'Have some honey on your bread. Perhaps it will sweeten your temper.'

She bit her lip. 'You mentioned my clothes. Do you mean you're letting me have them back?'

'Your case is downstairs at this moment.'

'And my money? My passport?'

'Not those.' The dark eyes glinted. 'Nor your plane ticket to England.' He looked at her, half-smiling, half-watchful. 'Are you really so eager to leave me?'

She shrugged again. 'There isn't a great deal to keep me here—now that you've got what you wanted.'

'And you did not?'

'Oh, naturally.' She sat down on the edge of the bed, and poured herself some coffee. 'It's always been an ambition of mine to be—deflowered by an expert. I shall remember it as the highlight of the trip.'

There was an electric silence, then he said silkily, 'But you have forgotten. It is my intention to supply you with a more tangible reminder of your stay here.'

Her cup clattered back on to the tray. She felt all the colour drain out of her face. Involuntarily her hand flew to the flatness of her stomach. 'No.'

'You have some reason for thinking you are immune?'

She had no reason at all, and she wished desperately she'd listened more closely to the information which would have told whether it was likely. She supposed it could be.

She had been so busy fighting her attraction to him, that she had indeed forgotten that last stark threat to make her pregnant.

He said, his tone dry, 'The idea does not seem to appeal to you. You would not like to carry my child under your heart?'

It was agonising to realise there was little she would like more, if only ... She snapped such thoughts off at the roots. They were futile, and could be heartbreaking.

She made herself meet his gaze, lifting her chin defiantly. 'I wouldn't carry it,' she said. 'In England, we have resources to deal with such problems.'

'But only within a certain length of time, I understand. How do you know I would let you go in time?'

She said in a low voice, 'Because I don't believe

that even you could be that cruel. You said you wanted my family to suffer? Just knowing that I was pregnant by a man they'd never met would be enough for that.'

The dark face was hard. 'Well, let us wait and see.'

She said almost inaudibly, 'Yes.' Then, more strongly. 'Could I have my case, please. I'd—I'd like to get dressed.'

'Then you shall.' From the doorway he looked back at her. 'Eat something, *pedhi mou*.' He sounded faintly mocking. 'To starve yourself now will solve nothing.'

She said coolly, 'I suppose not.' She reached for the bread, took a piece, added butter and honey, and bit into it, marvelling at her own outward calm.

But he was right about one thing, she thought as she listened to him go down the stairs. There was only one solution, as there always had been, and that was escape.

Back in her own clothes she looked and felt more like the Gemma of old, she decided, taking a critical look at herself in the mirror. He had left her alone to change, which she hadn't altogether expected, and when she heard him come back into the room, she tensed slightly, waiting for some sardonic remark. But although the dark eyes took in every detail of the plainly cut cream shift, and the low-heeled sandals which matched it, he said nothing.

He glanced at his watch. 'It is time we were going. It's a long drive.'

Gemma examined a fleck on one of her nails. She said, 'I've changed my mind. I'd prefer to stay here.'

'With Cerberus?' he asked mockingly.

'With anyone, or anything,' she said. 'I hope I make myself clear.'

'As the finest crystal,' he returned civilly, but she could detect an undertone of anger. He walked over to her and took her chin in his hand. He said, 'Do nothing foolish, my dove.'

She shrugged. 'What could I do? I imagine I'm still *persona non grata* in the village, you're taking the jeep, and I shall have my jailer. Getting my clothes back doesn't really make all that difference.'

He smiled rather grimly. 'You are wrong, believe me, *matia mou*. They make all the difference in the world.' He bent and kissed her on the mouth, then left the room and went downstairs.

Gemma unpacked her case, and put her things away, but in her own room, not the one they had shared. Defiantly, she shook out a simple broderie anglaise nightdress and arranged it on the bed.

She was just putting the last dress on the hanging rail, when she heard Cerberus bark below.

Andreas was in the living room waiting for her, his hand on the dog's collar. He said, 'Here is your companion.' He paused. 'Can I bring you anything from Aghios Nikolaos?'

'No thank you.' She would have loved some more books, but would have died rather than tell him so.

'A different brand of perfume perhaps?'

'No.' She glared at him.

For a moment it seemed as if he was going to say something else, but he merely shrugged, and went down the terrace steps, and presently she heard the jeep drive off.

She sank down on to the sofa, and began to cry

very softly, the tears running unchecked down her face and dripping on to her skirt.

She heard an anxious snuffling whine, and then Cerberus was beside her, pushing his formidable nose on to her lap, and presenting all the signs of a sheep in wolf's clothing.

She said brokenly, 'Oh Cerberus—I should hate him, but I can't. It's only been a couple of days, but it seems like a lifetime, and it will be too, because I'll love him until I die.'

She didn't seem to be making a lot of sense, but Cerberus seemed to understand, because he whined again and allowed her to put her wet cheek on top of his massive head. He smelled strongly of dog, and he was probably infested with fleas, but Gemma put her arm round his shaggy neck and hugged him and knew an odd comfort.

Presently she sat up, scrubbing the tears fiercely from her face with her hand. Andreas didn't give a damn about her. He was and always had been using her, as he'd made brutally clear, and it was no use sitting moping all day.

She got up, hooking two fingers into Cerberus' collar with what she hoped he would recognise as confidence. 'You and I,' she told him, 'are going for a walk.'

He couldn't have known the word, but perhaps he recognised the tone of voice, because to her amazement he trotted along obediently beside her. Once outside the house, she didn't even hold on to his collar any more. There was a slight contretemps outside the gate when Gemma turned towards the track up the mountain, when Cerberus clearly thought they should be going to the village, but that was soon resolved.

'You're a fraud,' Gemma told him pulling one of his ears. 'I let you terrify the life out of me yesterday, yet I bet at home you fetch people's slippers, and roll over and die for your master.'

He grinned, showing the kind of teeth nightmares are made of, and she said, 'And there again, perhaps not.'

The track proved to be very much as Andreas had said, only rather steeper and stonier. Gemma found it hard going. The stones kept slipping and rolling under her feet. Once she nearly fell, and another time twisted her ankle badly enough to have to sit on a boulder and swear at it.

Certainly it was the last sort of place that any pregnant woman should be scrambling about on, she thought, grimacing. She'd been thinking of Maria, but of course the same thing could apply to herself.

Could it possibly be true? She did some swift calculations, and realised it wouldn't be too long before she would have proof, one way or the other. It was a shattering realisation, underlining with humiliating force her own naïveté about the workings of her body and emotions. But then, how could she have expected her life to change so fast and so violently, she asked herself despairingly. Up to only a short time ago, her body had been her own private domain, and she'd been content for it to be so until she met the man she could love, until the tender leisurely courtship she'd envisaged took place, culminating eventually in a marriage when her white dress and veil would mean more than mere tradition.

She'd expected love to come to her like a gentle breeze blowing across the summer of her life—not a hurricane sweeping her crazily away, she thought helplessly.

She struggled up the last few yards of the track and emerged panting on to a small plateau. The view to the valley was dizzyingly spectacular, but was it this Maria came to see?

Beside her Cerberus barked excitedly, and took off towards what she'd first thought was a pile of stones under the cliff wall, but which Gemma now realised must be the remains of the shepherd's hut Andreas had mentioned.

It had been constructed out of the materials closest to hand, she thought as she approached. There was a low door, but no windows, and an apology for a roof made from brushwood.

Cerberus had vanished inside and was giving little muffled yelps, and she followed, bending to avoid cracking her head on what passed for a lintel. It was very dark inside, and it smelt of animals. Presumably on occasion the sheep and goats slept there along with their herders, she thought, wrinkling her nose, and this must be what was exciting Cerberus.

As her eyes became accustomed to the gloom, however, she began to realise the hut had been occupied and recently. There was a tin plate, still with traces of food, which Cerberus was investigating noisily, a water bottle, and reposing on a pile of scrub which had been pulled together in a corner to form a bed, a sleeping bag.

Gemma's mouth went dry suddenly. The pattern of the bag, dark blue with a red lining, was familiar. She half-knelt beside it, her fingers searching the lining just inside the zip until she found what she was looking for. She knew it was there, because she'd sewn it in herself, a long time ago, and not very neatly either. She looked down at the narrow strip of fabric, and the words 'Michael Leslie' danced before her eyes. Mike's sleeping bag. So he was here, living rough in this hut, hiding from Maria's family. She pressed her knuckles against her mouth like a frightened child. So this was why Maria was braving that awful scramble—because Mike was relying on her for food and other essentials.

She shivered. Had either of them considered what the consequences might be if Maria's relatives became suspicious of her daily jaunts and followed?

She remembered that stomach-churning drop to the valley floor, and felt sick. One of her main consolations had been that Mike was well away from Loussenas, out of immediate danger from Maria's justifiably resentful family.

She licked her dry lips. Yet here he was, within half a mile of the village, liable to discovery by anyone with the same measure of idle curiosity as herself.

And it hurt, too, to think that Maria must have told him she was at the Villa Ione and why, yet he'd made no attempt to help her, or even send her a message.

He must be terrified, Gemma thought, biting her lip. And he must have little faith that her sacrifice—that the vengeance already exacted—would be enough to satisfy the blow to the pride of Stavros and his family. He must know that he was in peril, too.

Cerberus lifted his head, whined sharply and was gone, his body darkly silhouetted against the sunlit doorway. At the same moment, Gemma heard the sound of a footstep, and rose sharply, her heart thudding unevenly. She said shakily, 'Mike?' and moved into the sunlight. For a moment it dazzled her, but not enough to make her think, even for a minute, that it was really Mike standing in front of her.

The hands which gripped her shoulders, hurting her, were only too familiar.

His voice shaken by rage, Andreas said, 'What in the name of God are you doing here?'

'I came for a walk,' she said defensively. 'I thought you were going to Aghios Nikolaos. Why did you come back?'

'Because I didn't trust you,' he said bitingly. 'And it seems I was right. When I found the house empty, I remembered the questions you'd asked about the mountain, and followed.' He shook her. 'You little fool, this is not the place for a casual stroll. You could have fallen—injured yourself—and for what—a glimpse of a wilderness?'

She dragged herself free. 'Thank you for your concern,' she flashed. 'Is it for me, or for the seed you're so egotistically sure you've planted in me?'

His eyes blazed at her, making her shrink away from him. 'How dare you speak to me in such a way . . .' He stopped abruptly, clearly fighting the loss of his temper. There was a silence, then he said, 'I ask again, Gemma, what are you doing here?' He looked past her to the hut, his eyes narrowing. 'Or must I guess?'

She said in a thread of a voice, 'No . . .' but before she could intervene, he was past her, bending his tall body beneath the low door. She waited, trembling with apprehension, as long minutes seemed to drag past.

He rejoined her, his face set and grim. He said softly, half to himself, 'So this is where he has been—all this time. If Stavros had known—if we had all only known.'

She said urgently, 'Andreas—don't tell anyone—please.'

His mouth curled. 'You can plead for him—this worthless brother of yours? When he has been hiding here like a coward, letting you pay the price of his folly?'

'Perhaps he doesn't know,' she said desperately. 'Perhaps he's only just returned.'

His glance was contemptuous. 'He has been there for days. Didn't you count the number of cigarette ends?'

She looked at him dazedly. 'Cigarette ends? But Mike doesn't smoke.'

He shrugged. 'Then he has started since you saw him last.'

'No,' Gemma said with conviction. 'He never would. He's a botanist—mad on ecology. He looks on cigarettes as a source of pollution—a health hazard. He wouldn't use them under any circumstances.'

His gaze was still sceptical. 'Fear can do strange things to a man.'

'Nor,' she said clearly, 'is he a coward.'

There was a brief tense silence as they looked at each other. Then Andreas turned abruptly, whistling to Cerberus who had retired to a safe distance and was sitting, watching them. 'Come.' His hand closed round hers. 'We will go down.'

Although she would have died rather than admit it, she was thankful he was there as she slid and slithered behind him down to firmer ground.

He didn't relinquish her hand, and she almost had to trot to keep up with his long stride. She was breathless and indignant by the time they reached the top of the terrace steps. He pushed her ahead of him into the house.

He said arctically, 'You have ruined your ridiculous shoes.'

Looking down, she saw that he was right. One of the straps on her sandal was hanging broken, and the leather was scuffed and spoiled. Her dress too was streaked with dust, and there were other marks on the skirt from where she'd knelt in the hut.

She said in a voice which quivered, 'I'll have to change.'

'Then do so quickly.'

She glared at him. 'Don't give me orders. Besides—I've hurt my ankle. I can't hurry.'

'Allow me to help,' he said. He picked her up in his arms as if she was a child, and carried her up the stairs to her room, setting her on her feet not too gently. His eyes scanned the rail of her clothes. He pulled out a dress, sleeveless and full skirted in glazed cotton and tossed it to her. 'Wear this,' he directed. 'I shall return in a few minutes. Be ready to leave with me then.'

She swallowed, fumbling for the zip of her dress. 'Where are you going?'

'To the village.'

'To—to tell them about Michael?'

He exhaled impatiently. 'That is not your concern.'

'Whatever he's done, he's my brother.' She slid the dress off her shoulders, letting it fall to the floor. She stepped out of the little heap of crumpled fabric, and walked across to him, putting a hand on his arm, raising her face pleadingly to his. He looked back at her expressionlessly, but she knew what he was seeing—her body, barely covered in the wisp of bra which lifted her breasts, the lacy triangle veiling her womanhood. She whispered achingly, 'Andreas—please don't give him away—for my sake. I'd do anything...' She paused, half-expecting him to draw her close, but he didn't move. She lifted her hand, sliding it inside the opening of his shirt, caressing the warm, hair-roughened skin with the tips of her fingers. She said again, 'Please . . .'

He touched her then, putting her away from him with a suddenness which robbed her of breath and sent the colour draining from her cheeks.

His eyes were cynical as they flicked over her. His voice sneered. 'Bribing me, Gemma *mou*? Then try offering me something I do not already possess.'

He walked past her to the door, and went out, leaving her humiliated and alone.

CHAPTER EIGHT

THEY travelled in silence. Gemma kept stealing sideways glances at him, but the dark enigmatic face revealed nothing.

She'd hurried into her clothes, expecting at any moment to see a group of grim-faced men with rifles pass the villa on their way to the hut, to hunt Mike down, but in the end Andreas had returned alone, walking slowly, clearly lost in thought, his face frowning as he stared down at the dusty ground. Perhaps they hadn't believed him, she thought, or maybe they were just waiting for him to get her out of the way before they started their search.

She wanted to ask what was going to happen, but couldn't find the words. And she couldn't plead with him again, she thought, the bitterness of shame sharp in her throat as she relived those few humiliating moments in the bedroom.

She had not, she realised, underestimated his skill as a driver, but her heart was in her mouth a few times as he manipulated the jeep round those dizzying hairpin bends. She found herself remembering James' cautious ascent, and had to resist an impulse to grab the side of the jeep to steady herself. In a way, she was almost grateful for that fast, relentless drive, because while she had the prospect of imminent death at the foot of some gorge to think about, she couldn't worry about Mike and what was going to happen to him when Stavros and his family caught up with him. Or, what was going to happen to her too, she reminded herself a little shakily.

She'd expected Andreas to take the broad national highway which carved its way across the island from Heraklion to Aghios Nikolaos, but instead, to her surprise, he turned the jeep on to a secondary road and began to climb again.

She ventured, 'I thought we were going to Aghios Nikolaos?'

'Later,' he said. 'There is something else I must do first.'

She recognised that he did not intend to tell her what this was, and she subsided into silence once more, turning her attention to the cultivated terraces and olive groves they were rapidly passing. Ahead of them she could see a cluster of roofs, and a church tower very white against the blue arch of the sky, and she felt the jeep began to slow as they entered the village street.

It was a pleasant street, lined with trees, the terraces of the single-storey houses which bordered it alive with flowers. Andreas pulled into the shade and stopped the engine.

Gemma asked, 'Shall I wait here for you?'

He shook his head. 'I don't know how long I shall be,' he said. 'There's a taverna in the square. Go and get yourself a drink.' He took some money from his back pocket and handed it to her, before striding away purposefully up the street.

She watched him arrive at his destination—a small pink-washed house, shaded by an enormous fig tree. Two women were sitting under the tree, clad in the traditional black, their heads bent over their embroidery. As he went in at the gate, they looked up, then rose to their feet, exclaiming in what seemed to be pleasure.

Andreas shook hands with them both with a certain amount of ceremony, then all three of them vanished into the house.

Gemma turned away in the direction he'd indicated as leading to the square, with a little mental shrug. They couldn't be part of his harem, she told herself ironically. Even from a distance, she could see they were both old enough to be his mother, if not his grandmother. So—perhaps they were something to do with his business. Maybe he was an entrepreneur in handwoven cloth and embroideries, and they were part of his workforce. And maybe too it was none of her business, she decided as she arrived in the square.

There was another surprise waiting for her here. It wasn't a large square, but it was a positive hive of activity. Outside the taverna long tables had been set up covered in snowy cloths, and people were milling around them adding cutlery, crockery and flowers, bringing chairs and laughing and talking at the tops of their voices.

The taverna owner seemed slightly harassed, but he brought the fresh lemonade she haltingly asked for. His English wasn't very fluent, but she managed to make enough of her questions understood to learn that there was a wedding. That the couple were in church that very moment, and that when they emerged there would be a big celebration.

Gemma said 'Oh?', and smiled and wished she'd stayed with the jeep after all. She felt very much as if she was intruding on a private occasion, and her fairness made her feel conspicuous, and deeply aware of the curious though friendly glances which were coming her way.

She lingered over her lemonade, wishing that Andreas would come and whisk her away, but by the time her glass was empty he still hadn't come to join her, and almost in desperation, she ordered another.

As the taverna owner set it down on the table, she heard him give a roar of pleasure and looking up she saw Andreas walking towards them, his face set and grim. At once he was surrounded by a grinning group of men, all vigorously shaking his hand and slapping him on the back.

Definitely an entrepreneur, and a successful one, Gemma thought judiciously. He probably kept the village supplied with work, but today he was annoyed because the two women had told him they couldn't manage some rush order.

It was some minutes before he disengaged himself and came to join her, dropping into a chair, and stretching his long legs in front of him.

He gave her a bleak look. 'Our trip to Aghios Nikolaos will be delayed,' he said expressionlessly. 'Hara and Petros are being married, and we are expected to stay and join the celebrations for a while.'

'But that's impossible,' Gemma protested.

His brows drew together icily. 'May I know why?'

'I should have thought it was obvious,' she said tightly. 'These are your friends, and it's a family occasion. I hardly think they'd welcome me if they knew the truth.'

'What truth is this?'

She bit her lip. 'That I'm—your mistress.'

He shrugged. 'You think not? Yet perhaps they are not as naïve, or as narrow-minded as you seem to suggest.'

In other words, they were probably quite used to seeing him with some enslaved female in tow, she thought raggedly.

He said on a mocking note, 'Don't look so stricken, Gemma *mou*. You are being asked to pass an hour or two in eating, drinking and dancing. Is that really so bad?'

Almost as bad as it could be, she thought. She didn't want to be with him like this, as if they were a couple and belonged together.

Besides, a wedding was altogether too intimate an occasion for them to share even on its fringe—too evocative of all the secret absurd dreams she hardly dared acknowledge even to herself.

'But perhaps the entertainment offered is a little too unsophisticated for your taste?' his voice continued remorselessly, flicking her on the raw. 'You were, after all, looking forward to the cosmopolitan delights of Aghios Nikolaos.'

She said unsteadily, 'Damn you, you know that isn't true. I'm looking forward to nothing.' As soon as the words were uttered, she regretted them, wondering if she had given away too much, but he seemed unaware of her slip.

'Not even to being reunited with your beloved brother? I thought you would be waiting eagerly to meet him again—almost as eagerly as I am myself,' he added grimly.

'Why?' she asked bitterly.

The firm lips were tautly compressed. 'So that I can be sure that justice has been done,' he said, half to himself.

'And how will you do that?' Her hands clenched together in her lap. 'By comparing scores—to ensure you've had me as many times as Mike had Maria?'

She could feel his anger as his mouth curled in a mirthless smile. 'An intriguing notion, Gemma *mou*. Are you now admitting that your brother is not the paragon you have always claimed? That you believe he did indeed seduce her and has been hiding like a coward on the mountain ever since, leaving you to pay the penalty?'

Gemma bent her head. 'I don't know what to believe any more,' she said wearily. 'All I know is that I'm not really in the mood for a celebration.'

'No more than myself,' he said coldly. 'Nevertheless, we must stay for a while at least. To leave when we have been invited would give offence, and these are good people.'

'Crete is full of them according to you,' she muttered, not looking at him. She sighed. 'All right then—we stay.'

She still felt agonisingly conspicuous as she sat and watched him move among the various groups who were gathering, seeing the pleasure and respect with which he was greeted, and wondering about it. He was still almost a total enigma to her, she realised unhappily. She'd begun to know his body intimately, but his mind was still closed to her.

This was the first time she'd seen him in association with other people—the first time she'd been obliged to think of him as a person in his own right with a life completely divorced from the Villa Ione and all its connotations. He had a family, friends, business associates while she—she belonged in a separate compartment of his life, and one that could be easily jettisoned when the time came, she reminded herself painfully.

She could hear music in the distance at first, then growing louder, and a few minutes later the musicians came into sight round the corner from the church, walking ahead of the bridal procession.

In spite of herself, Gemma felt her spirits lift at the intrinsic joyousness of it all. Everyone was happy, wreathed in smiles. The bride Hara was

plump and not dazzlingly pretty by any means, but
her dark eyes sparkled like the sun as she looked
adoringly at the thickset young man by her side,
and his protective air as he led her to the seat of
honour at the table enclosed them both in a kind
of beauty which went deeper than any surface
charm.

Everyone was moving to the tables now, taking
their places, but Gemma hung back feeling more
of a stranger with every second that passed.

Andreas said harshly, 'Do you mean to sit there
all day?' and pulled her to her feet in one easy
movement, his hand firm on her waist as he guided
her to a seat. People were grinning in welcome,
making room for them, and Gemma's hand was
shaken a dozen times or more. She was being
swept along on a tide of goodwill which was
almost overwhelming, absorbed into what seemed
a vast group of women clustering around her.
Their chattering voices rose and fell like birdsong,
and the fact that she didn't understand a word of
what they were seeing seemed irrelevant. With
little admiring noises, they stroked her blonde hair,
pointed to the fairness of her skin, and fingered
the fabric of her dress, making it clear to her that
she was welcome, and that they found her
beautiful.

She had no idea what, if anything, they made of
the fact she was there with Andreas. Probably it
was just her own over-sensitivity which made her
feel so wretched about the whole situation.

She found her glass being filled with wine, then
filled again. Great platters of lamb baked in the
oven with herbs and meltingly tender, were being
brought from the taverna, with bowls of salad, and
dishes of steaming fried potatoes fragrant with
lemon. In spite of her half-hearted protests, her

plate was heaped with food. Eat, she was urged
mischievously in sign language, because a strong
man like the *kyrie* needs a strong woman, they
added with laughter, and Gemma found she was
laughing too. That in spite of the agonies of
heartache and worry, her mouth was watering for
the food. And that never in her life had she tasted
anything so delicious.

He was sitting further along the table from her,
on the opposite side, among the men, and she
found her glance straying to him over and over
again. He didn't seem to be enjoying himself
particularly. He was smiling and joining in the
conversation around him with what was clearly an
effort, and in between his face still held that
brooding bleakness. Was it just business worries,
she wondered, or was the quarrel they'd had
earlier getting to him?

She bit her lip, remembering his anger with her,
his contempt. The memories hurt, and she wished
that the pain could be deep enough to stop her
loving him. She wished something could burn out
of her for ever and ever the agony of this one-sided
relationship—destroy it and make her whole
again.

The music which had been playing quietly all
during the meal suddenly swelled in volume,
taking on a more pronounced rhythm, and she
realised, as she was urged to her feet, that it was
time for the dancing. Amid laughter and hand-
clapping, the bridal couple led the way into the
middle of the square, and the others swarmed
around them forming an enormous circle, hands
joined. Gemma felt lost at first, her feet unable to
copy the intricate steps she was being shown, but
after a couple of circuits of the square, her body
began to adapt itself instinctively to the dipping,

swaying rhythm, and she was laughing, absurdly pleased with herself when the dance came to an end, and the rhythm changed.

Now, it was time to watch, because the men—or some half-dozen of them were dancing alone, and with a wrench of the heart, Gemma saw that Andreas was one of them.

Everyone around her was clapping, accentuating the beat of the music, and she joined in too, unable to help herself. It was very different, she discovered, from the exhibition dancing staged for tourists in the Heraklion tavernas. This was no folklore demonstration, but a joyous, strangely powerful assertion of their masculinity by men occupying what was still, primarily, a man's world. The dance expressed their pride in their strength and their virility with every sure, confident movement, the muscular bodies an extension of the music's rhythm. It was alien to anything Gemma had ever experienced, alien even to her own tentative beliefs about the equality of the sexes, yet it moved her to her soul.

This pride, this certainty about the world and his place in it was part of his birthright, she thought, her mind faltering a little at the realisation. That was why there was no self-consciousness about the way the Greeks danced. It was an expression of their belief in life itself.

She could feel tears springing in her eyes, and turned away hurriedly, afraid that someone would see. When she had control again, the dance had ended and another circle was forming, but this time she returned to her place at the table and sat sipping her wine.

She knew she was being watched suddenly, and turned her head. Her glance met his; locked. They could have been alone. It was as if every sight and sound around them had removed to some vague distance, enclosing them in a golden bubble of timelessness which, she knew dazedly, she never wanted to leave.

No one else existed. And she knew that no one ever would for her, and it made no difference at all that in terms of sanity they had known each other for such a brief time.

The passage of actual hours and days was only another irrelevancy, she realised with a kind of shock. And if at this moment, she was seeing him for the first time, she knew she would still want him as fiercely—a wanting that transcended mere physical desire.

She shared his bed, but what she wanted was to share his life, however alien to her, with utter completeness, and the depth and passion of that wanting frightened her, especially when she knew it applied to her alone.

There was no future in their relationship. None. And she was all kinds of a fool to even consider the possibility. She'd begun by fighting him. She'd even won some kind of hollow victory, then ruined everything by her rapturous, mindless surrender to his unexpected tenderness. He'd seduced her after all, she thought baldly, and she'd let it happen. In fact, she'd gloried in it, allowing herself to forget briefly exactly why he was taking her.

Only, she hadn't been permitted to forget for too long, she thought painfully.

Perhaps the harshness of his reminder to her of the stark reasons for his possession had been quite deliberate. Maybe, he was being cruel to be kind, stripping away any foolish illusions she might be harbouring about their relationship, and making her face reality.

He was an experienced man. She'd probably

betrayed her true feelings to him a dozen times as she lay in his arms—but never more so than at this moment, she realised with anguish.

With a supreme effort of willpower, she tore her gaze from his, concentrating her attention fiercely on the frankly unintelligible conversations going on around her, refusing with a kind of defiance to look his way again.

She'd succeeded so well that she almost jumped out of her skin when his voice beside her said almost laconically, 'It is time we were going.'

The dark eyes were aloof again, his face forbidding.

She said, 'Oh,' and paused. 'Then may I say goodbye. Everyone's been so kind to me . . .?' Her voice trailed away in appeal, and he nodded briefly before turning away, and striding off in the direction of the jeep.

They all seemed sorry to see her go. Even though verbal communication had been minimal between them, Gemma managed to establish that she was sorry too. One of the women darted away and returned breathlessly with a small flat package which she presented ceremoniously to Gemma. She could see she was expected to open it there and then, and did so. It was a tablecloth, she discovered, made of handwoven lace, produced with the skill and care of generations somewhere in this village. On the open market, it would cost a great deal, but this was a gift to her—a gift which it would cause offence to refuse.

And not just any gift either. The smiles and signs and gestures all around her were signifying that the present was intended for when she herself became a bride.

She was blushing painfully, her throat constricted as she managed, *'Efharisto—efharisto poli.'*

Her cheeks were still burning when she arrived back at the jeep. She'd bundled the cloth back into its wrapping, but all the same she was aware of Andreas eyeing it as she climbed into the passenger seat, his face coldly cynical as he did so.

'They have taken you to their hearts,' he said, as he started the engine.

'Yes,' she forced a smile. 'They shouldn't have done this.' She gestured almost helplessly towards her parcel. 'Obviously they'd made it to sell and . . .' She swallowed. 'I hope you didn't mind my accepting it.'

'Why should I mind?' His brows rose. 'I am glad you had the sensitivity not to offer to pay for it.'

'Did you think I would?' she demanded, stung.

He shrugged. 'It has been known. Your countrymen seem sometimes embarrassed by the generosity they are shown here, and try to respond by producing their cheque books.'

Gemma shook her head, 'Not me, I'm afraid,' she said too brightly. 'I priced some of the textiles during the first few days I was here, and a cloth like this would be totally beyond my means.'

'This job you have is poorly paid?'

Gemma shook her head. 'Not at all, but I can't afford to splash every penny I have on a holiday. I have to support myself when it's over, after all.'

'You live alone?'

'No, I live with my parents, but I pay my share of the bills. And I was thinking of finding a place of my own—in the autumn perhaps,' she added, remembering with a kind of amazement all the plans she'd been making in what seemed a lifetime before.

Hurriedly, she changed the subject. 'Where are we going now?'

'To Aghios Nikolaos.' His mouth curled a little.

'You will find it in complete contrast to the village we have just left.'

'And is that where you work? Where you sell your textiles?'

His sideways glance at her was sharp. 'What gives you the notion that I deal in textiles?'

She shrugged. 'It was just a guess. Those ladies you were visiting—I thought perhaps they might work for you.' She paused. 'I don't think I saw them at the wedding. Were they there?'

'No,' he said. 'They were not. Neither do they work for me in any way. I visited them because Soula used to live in Loussenas and I wanted news of her family.' There was sudden harshness in his voice. 'Does that satisfy your curiosity?'

She said stiffly, 'I'm sorry. I didn't mean to pry.'

'Does that mean no more questions?' he asked derisively, and she flushed.

'You ask enough,' she muttered defensively.

It was his turn to shrug. 'You are not obliged to answer,' he pointed out casually, as if it was of little interest to him whether she did or not, and Gemma subsided, biting her lip in chagrin.

At last, she said, 'If you're still angry about what I said this morning . . .'

'I am not,' he said briefly, and she was silenced again.

It was a long journey, and the broad national highway which cut its way across the island to Aghios Nikolaos although fast was not particularly interesting, Gemma decided. Nor was she overly impressed with the string of resorts which bordered the coast down to the Gulf of Mirabello. The Gulf itself was an intense shimmering blue as they descended towards Aghios Nikolaos. It looked almost unreal, Gemma thought. An artist's dream come to life with the bleached rock, and the dazzle of the buildings crowding almost to the edge of the dancing, glittering water.

Aghios Nikolaos was larger than she'd expected, and very much busier—the Crete of the tourist, with its streets lined with souvenir shops, offering leather and ceramics, and the crowded tavernas edging the harbour where pleasure boats and caiques jostled each other at their moorings.

After the seclusion of Loussenas, the noise of the traffic, the hubbub of voices and laughter from the people thronging the narrow streets seemed to batter at her ears.

She gazed around, trying to assimilate the cheerful, noisy charm of the place and caught sight of another glimmer of water.

She pointed. 'Is there an inner harbour?'

He shook his head. 'That is our so-called bottomless pool, where legend says Pallas Athene used to bathe,' he told her drily. 'I would not choose to do so myself.'

'Is it really bottomless?' Gemma craned her neck for a better view.

'It is deep enough,' he returned.

She was hoping he would stop and let her have a closer view, but to her disappointment he edged the jeep through the busy traffic round the harbour, emerging on to a broad promenade with hotels and tavernas on one side and the shining blue of the sea on the other, dotted with the sails of small boats and windsurfers.

He glanced at her. 'Don't you want to ask where we are going?' he challenged, faint amusement in his voice.

Gemma lifted her chin. 'It's really none of my business. I'm just enjoying the drive.' She paused. 'It's so wonderful to be allowed out of prison for a while.'

'Yet not every prisoner can boast a cell as comfortable as the Villa Ione.' The amusement was overt now. 'Or a jailer so aware of your needs,' he added cynically.

'So what is this?' she asked jerkily. 'My parole. Do you expect me to give my word I won't try and run away?'

'Is there really any need?' The words were softly spoken, but they burned her, because they told her quite unequivocally that he was aware of how she felt. That he knew that separation from him would be an agony for her. She could only pray that he would assume it was merely a physical infatuation.

She knew she should answer him somehow—snap back at him, try and build some defences, however precarious, but she couldn't think of a single thing to say. She wasn't even sure she could trust her voice. Instead, she concentrated her attention on the glamorous settings of the luxury hotels which fringed the outskirts of the little town.

The signposts indicated they were on their way to Elounda. It was one of the places she'd read about before she came—a little fishing village which had been rocketed to resort status by the popularity of the British television serial, *Who Pays the Ferryman*, which had been filmed there.

The road was climbing steeply, and when they reached the crest she almost cried out because the broad bay below them was so beautiful, the water shimmering from jade to turquoise, then melting to azure where it merged with the sky. There was a sprinkling of islands too, dominated by one eye-catching rocky mass.

Andreas said, 'That is Spinalonga. It was once a leper colony.'

Gemma shivered. Such a grisly reality seemed to

have no place in the fairytale vista ahead of her. 'How awful.'

'It is quite safe now,' he said. 'In fact it is an attraction for tourists. Boats visit the island regularly.' He paused. 'You don't approve?'

'I think it's a little morbid,' she said. 'After all you come on holiday to enjoy yourself—to escape even. It seems odd to deliberately seek out misery, even if it is in the past.'

'Yet you yourself visited Knossos. Do you believe that life there did not also have its dark side once?'

'No,' she said, with a little sigh. 'I suppose every age in history has its own brand of violence. But it wasn't all like that, I'm sure. It couldn't have been. The Lily-Prince for example . . .'

'Ah,' he said softly. 'Where I first saw you, Gemma *mou*.'

She bit her lip. 'I'd forgotten,' she lied.

He laughed. 'You did not know,' he told her, but in turn she could have told him that he was wrong. Even then her senses had warned her she was being watched, although in her wildest imaginings she could never have guessed why, or where it would lead.

He was signalling he was about to turn off the road. Leaning forward, Gemma saw a tall arched gateway surmounted by a display of international flags. There was a rope barrier across the gateway which a smartly dressed security man unlooped for them, saluting as they drove past.

'What is this place?' she asked.

'This is the Hotel Apollonissos,' he said laconically.

'Are you meeting someone here?'

'Several people,' he agreed. 'I hope that you will be able to entertain yourself in my absence. There are the usual water sports on the beach, or you could sun yourself by the pool, if you would prefer.'

'I think perhaps I'd better wait for you in the jeep,' she said.

'What nonsense is this?' He turned to her, frowning.

'No nonsense at all,' she returned levelly. 'I'm not dressed for the kind of activities you're talking about for one thing, and for another, I'd imagine, judging by the guard on the gate, that the management prefer to keep their facilities private for the use of guests only.'

'They are not quite as exclusive as that,' he said drily. 'You may bathe in the pool, or order a drink at the bar without fear of being thrown out, foolish one. As for your clothes——' he shrugged. 'That can also be arranged. The hotel has an adequate boutique.'

'Adequate for millionaires, I expect,' Gemma said stiffly, glimpsing through the trees and shrubs which bordered the drive they were traversing, smooth lawns stretching down to a ribbon of pale sand along the edge of the sea. 'Perhaps you've forgotten that I happen to be a working girl. The Hotel Ariadne in Heraklion is more my environment.'

'Why denigrate yourself, Gemma *mou*?' he asked coolly. 'If I had thought you would be out of place here, then I would not have brought you.'

The jeep rounded a corner, and Gemma saw the hotel itself in front of them, an imposing two-storey building, dazzlingly white in the sunlight.

Andreas drove under another archway, and brought the jeep to a halt in a small paved courtyard, fragrant with green plants growing in huge stone urns. The air felt refreshingly cool after the heat and dust of the long drive, and Gemma inhaled thankfully as she looked around her.

He sprang out and came round to the passenger side, his hands closing inexorably on her waist as he lifted her down. 'Come.'

She hung back reluctantly. 'I really don't think I should. It all looks incredibly upmarket and glamorous.' She looked down at her simple chainstore dress with a faint grimace. 'I shall be totally out of place.'

He frowned swiftly, and she tensed, prepared for some blistering retort. At last he said, 'What do you want from me, Gemma? Reassurances about how beautiful you are? Do you not know that you fill my eyes?' He pulled her towards him almost fiercely, and his mouth took hers in a hard, bruising kiss in which the simmering anger she sensed in him was more evident than passion. When he let her go, she had to resist an impulse to cling to him, and was glad she'd done so when he said coolly, 'Now come with me quickly, because I am already late for my appointments.'

He opened a door, and she found herself in a broad corridor, floored with marble, the exterior wall made of glass to give panoramic vistas of the gardens. She would have liked to have lingered, but his long stride gave her no chance, and she was breathless by the time they arrived in the foyer. While Andreas went over to the long reception desk, Gemma stood staring about her.

There were stairs, she saw, directing guests to an open-air restaurant on the first floor, as well as lifts, desks for car hire and tourist information and an imposing shopping mall opening off the foyer itself. There were few people about. Most of the guests would be outside, she thought, soaking up the afternoon sun and other delights. Inside, there were no raised voices or loud noises, or even canned music. The whole atmosphere was one of hushed, unhurried luxury, and it made Gemma sigh a little. How the other half lives, she thought ruefully.

Andreas came striding back. 'I'll take you down to the pool area,' he told her. 'Dimitris, one of the under managers, is there, and he will look after you, and see you have everything you need.'

Gemma shook his hand off her arm. 'I can look after myself. I don't need another jailer.'

His mouth thinned. 'You need a beating,' he said softly and furiously. 'It is fortunate for you that I do not have time to administer it. Now, while you are here, you will keep a guard on that wasp's tongue of yours,' he added grimly.

His hand closed round hers, and this time she knew she wouldn't shake him off without a struggle, so she let him take her, seething, out of the foyer on to an enormous sunny terrace, and down a narrow flight of steps in the corner on to the lawns beneath.

She was aware immediately that they were attracting attention. Every step they took was being monitored in some strange way from beneath the sun umbrellas they were passing between, and Gemma couldn't imagine why.

Unless everyone knew they weren't guests at the hotel, and their presence was being remarked and resented, she thought forlornly.

She began to hope they would find this Dimitris soon.

He turned out to be a short, stocky man, talking to the waiters at the poolside bar, and when he saw them coming towards him, Gemma saw his jaw drop visibly, although he recovered immediately and came towards them smiling, and holding out his hand in greeting.

Gemma felt absurdly self-conscious as she stood waiting while they talked to each other. She didn't understand a word of what was being said, but it sounded as if Andreas was giving instructions rather than asking any favours, she thought, surprised.

And then a new voice intervened, female, husky and speaking good but accented English. 'Andreas—where have you been hiding yourself all this time? We have all missed you.'

She was beautiful, Gemma thought detachedly, a real Valkyrie of a girl with flaxen hair, and a figure bordering on the voluptuous and shown off to the best possible advantage in a tiny leopardskin print bikini. She was smiling at Andreas radiantly, and at the same time managing to give Gemma a look from her vivid blue eyes which was both hostile and dismissive. A clever trick, Gemma found herself thinking, and one which the newcomer had got down to a fine art.

Andreas turned to meet her, his smile easy in response. He said, 'You flatter me, Helga. I am sure your life is too full, too interesting, for you to have even given me a thought.'

She gave a little gurgle of laughter. 'Then you are wrong. We were only saying at lunch how cruelly you have been neglecting us.' She came even closer, putting a hand on his arm caressingly. 'But it is good to see you because I have an invitation for you. Tomorrow is my father's birthday and we are having a special dinner to celebrate. Both he and my mother would be so glad if you would join us.'

Her smile was winning, her fingers curling possessively on his dark skin. Gemma, watching, was shocked by a predatory impulse to do her violence.

He said, 'If only it were possible, but to my infinite regret, I have engagements for several days.'

She pouted appealingly. 'They will be so disappointed. We have hardly seen you at all this year.' Her glance flicked to Gemma. 'It is not kind to desert your—old friends.'

'Have I done so?' He lifted her hand to his lips. 'Then I apologise. Convey my respects to your parents, and assure them I shall have the pleasure of dining with them one night next week.'

Helga's eyes were heavy with seductive meaning. 'That will be good. We shall all look forward so much . . .' She paused. 'Now, won't you introduce me to your little friend?'

As a put-down, it couldn't be bettered, Gemma thought as she shook hands politely and murmured something. Helga's eyes were all over her taking in every detail of the cheap dress, and the simple sandals, and letting Gemma know what she thought of them with one derisive flicker of an eyebrow.

Andreas was looking frowningly at his watch. He pulled Gemma to one side. He said in an undertone, 'I have to go.' He paused, the frown deepening. 'You will be all right?'

She said brightly, 'Never better,' and watched him walk away round the edge of the pool. It needed all the strength she possessed not to run after him, begging him to take her with him wherever he was going, and she was proud of the control that kept her standing where she was.

She didn't know what his relationship had been with the gorgeous Helga, although she could guess. And the fact that her parents seemed to be around would make very little difference either. She was beautiful, sexy and very determined—a potent combination, Gemma had to acknowledge.

And next week—when her plane had left for England—next week he had promised to dine with them—with Helga for dessert, no doubt, she thought, her nails digging convulsively into the palms of her hands.

And she was all kinds of a fool to feel so bitterly, grindingly jealous because she'd known all along that she only existed on the fringe of his life, their relationship, such as it was, purely temporary, born out of bitterness and vengeance.

And when it was over, Helga and others like her would be waiting . . .

And I'll be waiting too, Gemma thought achingly. Waiting for the rest of my life.

CHAPTER NINE

GEMMA lay under the sun umbrella, pretending to read. Dimitris had been endlessly kind, producing a lounger and umbrella for her as if by magic, providing a selection of the latest paperback bestsellers for her to choose from, insisting that she had a long cool drink. But he could not persuade her to accompany him to the hotel boutique and choose a bikini to sunbathe in. Kyrios Andreas, he kept repeating almost plaintively, had left instructions. Kyrios Andreas would not be pleased if they were disregarded.

Gemma, however, remained adamant. She did not want to swim, she told Dimitris mendaciously because the glittering turquoise water looked infinitely cool and alluring, and she preferred to stay in the shade.

At last he shook his head sadly, said that if she required anything, she had only to tell one of the waiters, and took himself off.

She knew she was being an idiot, but she couldn't help it. She was conscious all the time of Helga's sharp blue gaze following her every move from across the pool, and there was no way she was going to strip and reveal all her body's pallid deficiencies in front of that sneering, suntanned goddess. Compared with Helga, she wasn't just slim, but thin, she knew despondently, and under the circumstances she preferred to remain covered, no matter how hot it was.

She found she was stealing covert glances at Helga from time to time, despising herself as she did so. The German girl was spectacular and knew it, she thought drily, especially after she had casually discarded the top of her bikini. She wondered what Helga's parents, who looked portly, middle-aged and conventional, made of their glamorous daughter's antics, and decided after a few moments' observation that they regarded them with doting, uncritical fondness. And presumably if she wanted to spend part of her vacation in bed with a rich, sexy Greek that was all right too.

She bit her lip sharply. That kind of speculation was bad news. The last thing she wanted was to start building images of Andreas and Helga together, his darkness against all that golden splendour.

She tried to interest herself in her book. It was by one of her favourite writers, but the problems of the main characters seemed to pale into insignificance beside her own, and for once the plot failed to grip.

'Still all alone?' Helga asked with sweet malice. Without waiting for an invitation, she gestured to a passing waiter to put a vacant lounger next to Gemma's. She had her sunglasses with her, and a bottle of expensive oil. She looked as if she'd come to stay, as she stretched languorously on the lounger, and began to apply the oil to her full, firm breasts. 'It is wicked of Andreas to leave you for so long. But that is the way he is.'

She paused, and Gemma wondered drily whether she was supposed to say, 'Thanks for the warning.'

'Have you known him long?' Helga asked. 'And how did you meet?' She was eyeing Gemma almost incredulously.

Gemma said lightly. 'Not long. And I suppose you could say my brother brought us together.'

She could see Helga trying to work that one out, and failing, then the other woman said, 'You are here on holiday, one supposes.'

The supposition was correct, but what Helga really wanted to know was when she would be going home, and Gemma was damned if she was going to tell her.

She said, 'Yes, I've always wanted to come to Crete.' And launched into a spritely and specious account of the museums she'd visited and the antiquities she'd seen, sensing and enjoying her companion's rising irritation.

At last Helga interrupted shrilly, 'But you did not meet Nikolaides in such places. It is not possible. And you are not a guest in this hotel. Did you come on some package tour?' She made the idea sound like an insult, which was probably exactly what she intended.

And Gemma thought, 'I'm not the only one who's eaten up with jealousy. She'll be here when I'm gone, but she isn't sure of him.'

She said equably, 'No, I'm not staying here unfortunately. It's a beautiful place, isn't it. Do you stay here often?'

'We have stayed here each year since it opened,' Helga returned ungraciously. 'We spend usually a month, but sometimes it is longer.'

And you'd like it to be permanent, Gemma added silently. Well, you have nothing to worry about from me. I'm just passing through.

But all she said quietly was, 'It must be wonderful to have such freedom,' and saw with relief Dimitris almost hurtling towards them.

'Excuse me ladies,' he was smiling smoothly, the polite managerial mask well in place. 'But Kyrios Andreas would like you to join him in the penthouse, *thespinis*.'

She got up thankfully. She looked down at Helga, smiling faintly into the lovely, sulky face. 'Goodbye, *fraulein*,' she said politely. 'It was good to meet you.' It was certainly salutory, she added wryly.

Helga's smile in return was small and hostile. '*Auf wiedersehen*. And you may tell Andreas that if he wishes to change his mind about dinner tomorrow night, he need only arrive.' She paused. 'He will be more than welcome.'

'I'll tell him,' Gemma agreed calmly, and walked away.

As they went into the hotel, Dimitris said, 'I hope Fraulein Gretz has said nothing to upset you, *thespinis*. Her father is a very wealthy man, an industrialist from Stuttgart, and she is an only child who gets very much her own way.'

'And is consequently spoiled rotten,' Gemma concluded for him. 'I'd rather worked that out for myself.'

'She can be difficult,' Dimitris conceded discreetly. 'And Kyrios Andreas was not pleased when he saw she was talking to you,' he added.

She failed to see why, although she didn't say so to Dimitris. There was nothing Helga could have told her that she hadn't been able to work out for herself.

They didn't use the public lifts, to her surprise. Dimitris unlocked a door in the reception area, revealing a short passage leading to another, smaller lift.

'This goes straight to the penthouse,' Dimitris said, pressing a button.

Gemma was totally at a loss as the lift ascended. 'So, what's up there?' she asked. 'Offices?'

'Just the boardroom, *thespinis*, and the apartment that Kyrios Andreas uses when he is at the hotel.'

'And does he stay here often?' she asked bemused, wondering what a permanent penthouse suite would cost in a hotel as luxurious as this.

'As often as he can, *thespinis*. Kyrios Nikolaides takes a close interest in the running of all his hotels, as his father did before him.'

She felt dizzy, as if the walls of the lift were closing round her. She said breathlessly, 'I don't quite understand, Dimitris. Are you saying this hotel actually—belongs to—to Kyrios Andreas— that he's the owner?'

As the lift doors opened, Dimitris gave her a slightly reproachful look. 'But of course, *thespinis*. How could you not know?'

'How indeed?' Gemma said ironically.

They passed the boardroom. She glimpsed a long polished table, and two secretaries gathering up papers. Then Dimitris was knocking at a door, and it opened and Andreas was standing in the doorway so close that she could have touched him, and yet in another way, they had never been further apart.

Her smile as she looked at him was forced, and she saw that he knew it, his eyes narrowing as she went past him.

It was a beautiful room, full of sunshine and colour, and light years away from the simplicity of the Villa Ione. There were huge windows on two sides giving panoramic views of the bay and the hotel gardens, including the environs of the pool. So that was how he knew Helga was with me, she thought.

She said in a wooden voice, 'Your hotel is fantastic. What a fool you must have thought me, chattering on about textiles.'

'I have never thought you a fool, Gemma.' His voice was quiet. 'Would you like some coffee? Or there could be tea if you preferred.'

'Or even champagne cocktails.' She went on staring out of the window as if the view fascinated her.

'Those too,' he agreed, sounding faintly amused. 'Is that what you would like?'

She shook her head. 'Coffee would be fine,' she said huskily. She paused. 'I can see why you were so sure the authorities would believe you, and not me. Kidnapping isn't the kind of thing you associate with respectable hotel owners.' She bit her lip. 'From what Dimitris says I gather you have a few of them.'

'There is another at Rethymnon,' he said. 'As well as those on Rhodes and Corfu.'

'The Nikolaides chain,' she said faintly. 'I should have realised when Fraulein Gretz mentioned your name. But even then I didn't make the connection.'

'You have heard of the hotels?' He sounded surprised.

'Heard, yes,' she said. 'But I never expected to set foot in one.' She smiled brightly. 'Another experience to treasure when I go home next week.'

There was an enormous sofa, like a divan, piled with cushions. He sat down and began to pour the coffee which was waiting on a low table.

He said, 'I think your return home is something we need to discuss.'

Her mouth was dry. 'You—you mean to keep me here?'

He shook his head. 'On the contrary, Gemma *mou*. I think it would be best if you went home almost at once. Tomorrow, if a suitable flight can be arranged.'

She took the cup he handed her. Her fingers didn't shake, which was amazing when she considered that her life had just fallen in ruins about her.

She said, 'Tomorrow would be perfectly convenient, I'm sure—for everyone.' She drank some coffee, and nearly scalded herself, but she kept smiling. 'You'll be able to attend Herr Gretz's birthday party. Your—Helga asked me to tell you the invitation was still open.'

'That is hospitable of her,' he said.

'I thought so too,' she said. In spite of the air conditioning, it was hot in the room, and yet she was so cold that any moment her teeth could start chattering. 'Do you think there's any chance of a reservation tomorrow?'

'I'll call down to our travel desk,' he said. 'Ask them to make some preliminary enquiries. It may be possible to transfer the unused portion of your return ticket.'

It all sounded very efficient, and she supposed she should thank him, but it was difficult to find the words when she was dying inside. She knew a terrible destructive impulse to throw herself at him—into his arms—down at his feet and plead with him not to send her away. And perhaps he sensed the loneliness in her, and the despair, because he said, quite gently, 'Gemma, believe me, it is necessary that I do this. I wish it was possible to explain fully.'

To explain what? That between her and the glamorous daughter of a wealthy German industrialist there was no contest?

And then, unbidden, from somewhere at the back of her mind, she saw the shepherd's hut, and an icy fear gripped her.

She said sharply, 'It's Mike isn't it—something

to do with him—and you don't want me to be here when it happens?' She ran her tongue round her dry lips. 'Or has it happened already? Your friend Stavros—has he found Mike? Harmed him?'

'No.' Andreas got to his feet and came to her. His arms went round her, but she stayed rigid in his embrace. 'It is not that, I swear. They would have to harm me first. But I have done you a great wrong, Gemma, and somehow I need to make amends. You must understand that.'

She shook her head wearily. 'I don't understand anything, and I haven't—not from day one.' She moved away from him, because even though there was only comfort in his embrace, her body was crying out for him just the same. 'Perhaps you'd phone about my ticket now.'

'Yes.' There was a phone on the table next to the tray, and she watched him lift it and dial a number. She didn't understand a word of the brief conversation which followed, but she felt that the sound of it would be imprinted on her brain forever.

He said, 'Kostas will phone us back as soon as he has news.'

'That's good.' She took a breath. 'It's a pity you didn't put my case in the jeep this morning. Then there would have been no need to go back to the villa.'

He shrugged. 'No problem.' He sounded casual to the point of indifference, she thought dazedly. The passionate lover who had caressed every inch of her body with his mouth and hands might never have existed.

But perhaps he never had, at that. Perhaps there had only been the cold-blooded avenger of Maria's honour, a role which he had not enjoyed, and now wished to forget with as little trouble as possible.

He talked of amends, but wasn't it more likely that, having exacted his vengeance, he was bored with her, and wanted to get his life back to its normal tenor?

She had known it would happen, expected it, but dear God, not so soon, she thought wildly.

She hurried into speech, trying to find a safe subject. 'This is a fascinating apartment. I'm surprised you can ever bear to leave it.'

'It's useful, but it does not afford a great deal of privacy,' he said drily. 'Would you like some more coffee?'

'No, thank you,' she said politely. She had hardly touched what she'd had, the taste of it as bitter as gall in her mouth.

She hurried into speech again. 'Could I see the other rooms?'

His brows lifted. He said coolly, 'It will be my pleasure.' He paused. 'Shall we start with the bathroom?'

She wouldn't have cared if he'd offered to show her the garden shed. She didn't want to see any of the apartment, but she had to say something, do something to fill this terrible aching void while she waited to hear whether she was being flown out the next day.

The bathroom was fantastic, tiled in black and gold with a huge sunken bath, and she couldn't think of a thing to say about it, so she made approving noises. The bedroom was vast too, the bed which dominated it covered by a spread of Cretan design in shades of blue and crimson.

Gemma stood in the doorway of the room and stared at it. Andreas was standing behind her, so close to her that she could feel the warmth of his body penetrating the fabric of her dress. She remembered the night she had stood on the terrace at Loussenas listening to the music from the village and the way his lips had caressed her neck and his hands touched her breasts. She was on fire for him, longing for him to draw him to her again with a depth of yearning which was physically painful. She wanted to turn into his arms, to feel his mouth on hers, parting her lips with passion. She wanted him to carry her to that bed.

But no amount of wanting could make it so, she discovered.

Instead, she heard him say, 'That completes the tour,' and her senses told her he had moved away back into the living room. After a moment, she did the same, avoiding his gaze, aware that her cheeks were unnaturally flushed.

It was almost a relief when the phone rang. Andreas lifted the receiver and listened, his face expressionless.

Then he nodded, uttered a swift word of thanks and put the phone down. He said, 'It is settled then. There is a plane just after four in the afternoon. You are booked on to it.'

Her mouth felt so dry suddenly, she was afraid her lips might crack. She said, 'Thank you. How— how will I get to the airport?'

There was an edge of impatience in his voice. 'I will take you there.'

'That's very kind of you,' she said politely. 'But I don't want to put you to any trouble, or inconvenience.'

His mouth tightened and he did not reply.

Gemma walked over to the other window, and stood rigidly staring out, fighting back tears with all her strength. He couldn't wait to be rid of her, it was evident, and all she had to ensure now was that she took her departure with some dignity. And bursting into tears, or revealing any other emotional weakness would be about as undignified as it was possible to get, she told herself.

At last he asked, 'Would you like to have dinner here, or return to the villa?'

Not looking at him, she said, 'Do you mean—actually here, or . . .?'

He said curtly, 'I meant in the restaurant. However, if you have no particular preference, it might be better if we returned to Loussenas.'

She said colourlessly, 'I would prefer that, too.'

'Then we had better be leaving.' He picked up the paperback she had brought up from the pool. 'Is this yours?'

She said, 'Dimitris gave it to me. I'd like to keep it to read on the plane, but naturally I'll pay you for it, when I get my money back.'

He said icily, 'You are all consideration. But perhaps you will accept it from me as a gift, as I understand you would take nothing else.'

She looked away. 'Just as you wish,' she said dully.

'We will not, I think, discuss my wishes.' His tone was grim. 'Now let us go.'

The sun had set by the time they reached Loussenas, and the Villa Ione was full of shadows. Andreas moved about lighting the lamps, but the shadows were still there, inside her, and she stood watching him, her arms wrapped across her body, hugging herself as if she was cold.

He said, 'Are you hungry?'

She thought, 'Only for you' but naturally she did not give the thought utterance. She shook her head. 'Not—really.'

'Then I suggest you get some rest,' he said. 'You have done a lot of travelling today, and you have another long journey to face tomorrow.'

She swallowed, lifting her chin. 'And—you?'

He turned away, making some adjustment to the shutters. 'I have to go down to the village,' he said at last. 'I will try not to disturb you when I return.'

If he had struck her across the face, the rejection could not have been more painful, or more final.

She licked her dry lips. 'To use your own words—you're all consideration,' she said tonelessly, then turned away and went upstairs.

From her window, she watched him walk slowly towards the village, his head bent, never glancing back even once. She shivered almost convulsively. Bitterness, anger, passion—she could have met all those, but not this chilly remoteness, telling her more plainly than any words that she had nothing to hope for from him.

As if I ever had, she thought wretchedly. That incredible sensual sweetness he had brought her the previous night had meant nothing to him. He'd made her respond, because his pride demanded it, that was all, but she was not and never had been 'his woman'. And now, she was an inconvenience, and an embarrassment on the edge of his life.

She took the clothes she had unpacked only a few hours before and thrust them into her case anyhow, humiliated tears burning behind her lids.

Then she showered and put on her nightdress, and got into bed, and lay staring into the gathering darkness. She felt weary to her bones, but her mind and senses were awake and crying out.

In a few short days her life had totally changed. She had totally changed. The self-contained girl, in charge of her emotions, in charge of her future, no longer existed, and she couldn't even be sorry.

Her hand slid wonderingly to the flatness of her abdomen. Perhaps the changes in her life would be more far-reaching than she could ever guess. She hoped there would be a child, in spite of the grief this would inevitably cause her family. And although the baby would have been conceived in an act of vengeance, it would be brought up in love no matter what the difficulties. She would manage somehow, and she would manage alone. She wouldn't use the baby as an excuse to contact Andreas again, as a fragile chain to keep him bound to her at any level of obligation. About that, she was adamant. When her plane left tomorrow, that would be the end—a break as clean as an amputation.

She sighed, her body twisting restlessly on the bed. But that was for the following day, and she had a long lonely night to get through somehow.

She had no idea how many hours had passed, but she was still wide awake, her mind treading the same painful tracks, when she heard him come back.

She listened to him moving about, then, her whole being tensing hopefully, expectantly, heard his footsteps on the stairs. She waited, staring at the door, willing him to come to her, her body one wild cry of yearning.

But without pause, without even hesitation, he went past her door and into his own room.

With a smothered groan, Gemma rolled over on to her stomach and lay still.

She lay for a long, dragging time, her pride, her self-respect fighting a bitter losing battle against the unending clamour of her senses.

At last, she slipped from the bed, and went out of the room, crossing the narrow passage to his door. It was closed, and she opened it quietly and went in.

He was awake too, and he turned his head slowly and looked at her, standing in the brilliance of the moonlight.

He said quietly, 'Go back to your room, Gemma. Go back now.'

She shook her head. 'No, Andreas *mou*. You're sending me away tomorrow, and I accept that, but let me have tonight.'

There was a taut silence, then he said harshly, 'You do not know what you are asking.'

'Oh, but I do.' She smiled, her mouth tremulous. 'You—you taught me too well, perhaps. Don't make me spend the rest of the night alone.' She paused. 'I'll never ask you for anything else—I swear it. No—demands on any grounds. But let me stay with you now.'

'Oh, God.' His voice was hoarse. 'Gemma—*agape mou*—I have done you the greatest wrong it is possible for a man to do to a woman. How much else do you want me to bear on my conscience?'

'Why should there be guilt?' she asked. 'Unless—you don't want me?'

He flung back the sheet and came across to her, his arms sliding round her body, fiercely, bruisingly.

'Not want you?' His voice almost broke. 'My sweet fool, how could I not want you?'

His fingers slipped under the narrow straps of her nightdress, pushing them from her shoulders, tugging them downwards until the garment lay in a white cloud on the floor. Then he lifted her into his arms, and carried her to the bed.

She was wild for him, the brush of his naked body against her own filling her with sensuous urgency. Her hands slid over his burning skin, paying tribute to the strength of him, the sheer animal grace, echoing without inhibition the passionate exploration his own fingers were making of her.

His head bowed to her breasts, his mouth taking one rosy nipple, then the other into sensual captivity, teasing the hardened sensitive peaks with his tongue until she moaned in pleasure and pleading.

He laughed in his throat. 'Patience, my dove, my tigress,' he told her huskily.

His mouth moved downwards over her trembling flesh, trailing fire, bringing every last sense to shattering, responsive life, making her shudder with delight.

His hands slid under her hips, lifting her towards him, silently demanding her acquiescence in the most intimate kiss of all, and she had neither the strength nor the will to deny him, her body convulsing in a shock of pleasure, a soundless scream tearing at her throat as his mouth possessed her.

She was mindless, dazed and rapturous with sensation, consumed by a sweet flame she had never dreamed existed, her body arching towards him, her head thrashing from side to side on the pillow. He moved, his body covering hers, glorying in the completeness of her acceptance of him, and she whispered her need in little broken words as she welcomed him into her, and went with him down the brief, explosive path to their mutual consummation.

And when it was over, she turned pliantly into his arms, pillowing her cheek against his sweat-dampened chest, and they slept.

And woke and made love again with slow, passionate intensity as the night began to take on the shimmer of the day. She clung to him, her hands raking at the smooth skin of his shoulders, the harsh hurry of her breathing matching his, her body poised on the edge of ecstasy, and realised with a kind of anguish that this was the last time she would ever fall through the stars to earth with him, and this agony of pleasure was their farewell to each other.

CHAPTER TEN

GEMMA woke first. For a long moment, she lay watching him, as if every line of that darkly arrogant face and strong, lithe body wasn't already committed to her memory, then moving very carefully so as not to disturb him, she slid out of his encircling arm, and out of bed.

This last time, she would make breakfast for them.

She picked up her discarded nightdress and slid it over her head. Although there was no one but himself to see, she still felt oddly shy about appearing naked in front of him.

She went silent and barefoot downstairs, and out into the kitchen, but the bread had not arrived. She filled the kettle and set it on the stove to boil. Later, she knew there would be pain as she faced the fact they would never meet again, but now, still wrapped in the aftermath of their lovemaking, she felt oddly at peace with herself.

And the sound of footsteps on the terrace, entering the villa was a disruption, although an expected one.

She turned her head, and called, 'Maria—I'm out here.'

Silence. She frowned a little moving towards the door. 'Maria?' Then stopped dead, her hand flying to her mouth with shock.

Michael stood just inside the dining room, his face a picture of stunned incredulity. He said on a whisper, 'Gemma? What the hell . . .?'

A wave of burning colour seemed to sweep up

from her toes, as she looked back at him. She could hear sounds of movement upstairs, and realised Andreas must have woken. At any moment, he could come down and find them . . .

She said hoarsely, 'Mike—you've got to get out of here, now. Which way did you come? Did they see you in the village?'

He looked at her as if she was mad. 'I don't know whether they did or not. What's the matter with you? And what are you doing here? Didn't you get my last letter?'

'Probably not,' she said shakily. 'But we haven't time to talk about that now.'

'Well, we need to talk about a few things,' he said austerely. 'For one, did you ask anyone's permission before moving in here? It's not for hire, you know. It's privately owned by some hotel tycoon called Nikolaides . . .'

'I know,' she interrupted hastily. 'And he mustn't find you here.'

'I've got permission,' he told her impatiently. 'Stavros, who's the head man in the village is a great friend of this Nikolaides and . . .'

'But not a great friend of yours—not any more.' She swallowed. 'Mike, I know about you—and Maria. They all know, and it's not safe for you to be here, believe me.'

He disengaged himself from his rucksack, dropping it to the floor with a thud. 'Oh, Maria,' he said casually. 'What's the little idiot been doing now?'

'Don't play games,' Gemma said bitterly. 'She's pregnant, and don't pretend you didn't know.'

He shrugged. 'Oh, I knew all right.' He sounded exasperated. 'But hell, I thought she'd be safely married by now. What's been the snag?'

Gemma looked at him, appalled. 'The snag,' she

said cuttingly, 'as you so winsomely put it, was her fiancé, who was understandably reluctant to take on someone else's child.'

'Not him,' he dismissed. 'I meant Kemal. I went to Chania to find him, and he was coming straight here to get her to marry her, even if it meant running away together. Don't tell me it's all gone wrong?'

From behind him, Andreas said grimly, 'Yes, my friend, it has indeed all gone wrong—very wrong.'

Mike swung round to face him, initial surprise giving way to wariness as he registered the fact that Andreas had clearly just emerged from the shower, and was wearing nothing but a towel draped round his hips. At once, his glance travelled swiftly and sharply towards Gemma as if assimilating her own lack of attire, and his expression changed to an amalgam of embarrassment and condemnation.

He said, 'Just who the hell are you? And what is my sister doing here with you?' He sounded defensive and rather young.

'Do I have to spell it out for you?' Andreas asked drily, but his tone held none of the triumph Gemma had expected from him now that he and Mike were actually facing each other.

Mike flushed. 'I suppose not,' he said with constraint. He didn't look at Gemma again, but the back of his head spoke volumes of disapproval and more.

'I have been hoping you would return,' Andreas went on almost conversationally. 'And so, I understand, has your friend Kemal, who has spent an uncomfortable time camping out in a shepherd's hut on the mountain.'

Mike frowned. 'What on earth for?'

Andreas' mouth curled. 'The car he was using broke down on the way here, and he had to abandon it, and with it, his romantic plans for an elopement in the teeth of Stavros and his family. Instead, he had to hide on the mountain, eating as and when Maria could smuggle him food, and waiting for you to come to his rescue yet again.'

Mike groaned. 'If that isn't typical,' he began furiously. 'I was sure it would be all cut and dried by now. God knows, I never wanted to get involved in the first place.'

'Then why did you?' the cool voice asked inexorably.

Mike grimaced. 'I met Kemal in Chania ages ago. He seemed a bit of a loner at first, but we used to eat in the same places, and got talking, and eventually he told me about this girl he was in love with from one of the villages. Only, he said, her family wouldn't hear of it because his father was Turkish, and his mother was considered to have disgraced herself by such a marriage. It didn't seem to make a lot of sense to me, but I felt sorry for him, and for her too, when I found out her family were planning to marry her off to some guy she hardly knew. But in the meantime, she was in Chania, working in some relative's hotel as a waitress, and Kemal was meeting her on the quiet.'

Gemma stood as if frozen, listening to the story unfold, hearing it at last make a kind of terrible sense in her mind. Maria's lover was part-Turkish, she thought, which would arouse all kinds of ancient enmities.

'It seemed an ideal arrangement,' Mike continued, 'until the family got suspicious and she was whisked back here to Loussenas. Kemal couldn't follow at once—her father had banned him from his house a long time before, and naturally he was nervous about showing himself in the village, but he knew I was planning to come to this area anyway to do some research, so he asked me to keep an eye on Maria—make sure she was all right, and that they weren't pushing this marriage at her.'

He paused. 'I could see why he wanted to steer clear of her father. Stavros is a formidable guy, although he was kindness itself to me, arranging for me to use this villa. I really didn't like deceiving him, especially when I found Maria was expecting me to act as a go-between for Kemal and herself. It was just after this that she found out about the baby. She knew all hell would break loose and she begged me to go to Chania and tell Kemal. Well,' he shrugged, 'I felt I couldn't refuse under the circumstances, and as it happened I'd just had a letter from a university mate of mine, Chris Hennessey, saying he and a couple of others were planning to take a caique across to Karpathos, and did I want to join them?' He shrugged again. 'You don't turn down a chance like that, so I wrote to Gem, telling her to postpone her trip for a month or so. It never occurred to me she'd come anyway,' he added in a tone of faint injury.

'The letter must have been delayed,' Gemma said. 'I never received it.'

Michael turned and looked at her, flushing a little. 'Okay, these things happen. But coming here is one thing. Getting yourself—involved with some guy you can only just have met is quite another.' He stopped swallowing. 'Gem, this isn't like you. It would just about kill the parents if they knew.'

She bit her lip. 'Do you plan to tell them?'

'No, of course not,' he denied heatedly. 'But all the same . . .'

'You must not blame your sister in any way,' Andreas said calmly. 'Your quarrel is with me, and me alone. Because of the lies Maria told her family after you had left the village, they believed you were the father of her baby.'

'I was?' Mike sounded outraged. 'But that's insane. I mean—she's a nice enough girl, I suppose . . .'

'Nevertheless, that is what she told them, and they believed her. She was terrified that if she told the truth, Kemal might come to some harm. As you said, Stavros is indeed a formidable man, and he did not take this damage to his daughter's honour lightly. He wanted—vengeance.'

'So?' Mike's eyes narrowed sharply.

'So—the letter Gemma wrote to you giving details of her travel plans was found in your room. And to avenge Maria's honour, and bring shame on you, as you, it was thought, had disgraced Stavros and his kin—to punish you, I—took your sister.'

There was a long silence, then Mike said unevenly, 'Christ.' He swung round on Gemma. 'Gem—does this bastard mean he—raped you?'

Her face burned. 'No.'

Her brother's usually gentle face was ugly suddenly, and she moved to him swiftly, gripping his arm, interposing herself between the two men. She said softly and urgently, 'Mike—I can't explain—I have no excuse at all, but it—wasn't rape. It—happened, and now it's over—all over, and I'm leaving this afternoon for home. And there's no need for anyone to know anything unless you tell them.'

His voice shook. 'Oh, my God.'

Andreas broke in swiftly, 'There is no name you can call me that I do not deserve. Nothing you can say, that I have not already told myself a hundred times. But by the time I came to suspect the truth, it was already too late.' The dark face looked suddenly haggard. 'At first, I couldn't believe we had all been so wrong. I thought Kemal had gone to the Turkish side long ago to join his father's people. So yesterday I spoke to his mother and his aunt, who live now in a village a little way from here, and they told me he had never left Crete. They told me, too, he was planning to marry, and would be bringing his bride to them soon.'

Gemma said half to herself, 'The house with the fig tree.'

He said quietly, 'Yes.' There was a long pause, then he said, 'There is only one way in which I can now make amends for Maria's lies and the terrible harm they have caused. In the absence of her father, I ask you Kyrios Michalis, for your sister in marriage.'

In a voice she barely recognised as her own, Gemma said, 'No,' violently.

One long stride brought Andreas to her. He took her by the shoulders, turning her to face him. 'What do you mean?' he demanded harshly.

'Exactly what she says,' Mike cut in. 'And who can blame her? Anyway, I'm here now, and she doesn't have to do anything you say again, you scum, no matter how many times you may have had her in your bed. She can do better than you, God knows, any day of the week.'

Gemma said softly, 'Mike—this is Andreas Nikolaides.'

And watched his jaw drop in shock. But he made a stout recovery. 'To hell with that. I stand by every word I've said. The best thing Gemma can do about a swine like you is forget you ever existed.'

'And is that what you wish, Gemma?' His hands were still holding her inexorably, his eyes grim as he stared down at her.

Somehow, she found the strength to tear herself free. 'Yes,' she said in a thread of a voice. 'I'm tired of obligations and—and honour, and making amends. I just want to get out of here—away from you. I want to go home.'

'So you keep away from her from now on,' Mike added fiercely. 'Leave her alone, or you'll have me to reckon with.'

Andreas' face was sardonic suddenly. He was taller than Mike, heavier, stronger, more muscular in every way. Mike's threat was on the face of it absurd, and Gemma cringed from the crushing words she was sure would come in reply, but all Andreas said was, 'Very well,' before turning and walking away, leaving brother and sister together.

The inside of her lower lip felt raw. Her teeth had almost met in the soft, moist flesh.

She said in a high, strained little voice, 'I think I'd better get dressed.'

'Don't you think we should talk first?' His face was unhappy as he studied her. 'I can see now why you wanted to get rid of me so damned quickly. You didn't want me to catch you with your millionaire—stud.'

Gemma winced, 'Don't.'

He flushed. 'I'm sorry, love.' There was real compunction in his voice. 'That was a lousy thing to say. But I can't relate you to—all this. You've admitted yourself he didn't have to use force, for God's sake. And yet you're no raver, and never have been. I—I just don't understand any of it.'

She said wearily, 'Nor do I, believe me. But I was not trying to chase you away because I was ashamed of anything I'd done. I was frightened for you, that's all. You see, I didn't know this Kemal even existed.'

For a moment he looked bewildered, then a quick frown spread. 'You don't mean you actually believed Maria's ridiculous lies about me?'

'No, I don't think I ever did,' she acknowledged quietly. 'I said from the first, that you'd never have seduced anyone and left them in the lurch. But—Andreas did believe it, and so did Maria's family. And I couldn't take it for granted that what Andreas had done to me would be enough for them.' She shuddered. 'I thought in spite of everything they might—kill you.'

He muttered something awkwardly, and patted her arm, then looked past her into the kitchen. 'There's a kettle there, boiling its head off,' he said with an attempt at lightness. 'Go and get some clothes on, and I'll make the coffee.'

She gave him a grateful smile and escaped upstairs.

Andreas was waiting in her room. He was dressed, she registered numbly, in smoothly tailored slacks, and a casual navy shirt which he was still buttoning. He looked at her grimly.

'Have you nothing to say to me?'

'What is there to say?' She dragged a tan-and-white striped dress out of her case, and tossed it on to the bed. 'Except that I realise now why you were having such pangs of conscience about me.' She paused. 'When did you realise this—Kemal was the one involved?'

'When you told me your brother did not smoke, I wondered,' he said. 'But even so, I was only guessing at first. I knew, of course, there had been some talk of love when they were both younger, which Stavros had forbidden even then. And when his mother moved from the village, I supposed that would be the end of it.'

'So, what will happen now?' she asked tightly. 'Does Kemal have a sister, or will Stavros and his men merely hunt him down in the mountains?'

'Neither.' A tiny muscle jumped beside his taut mouth at her bitter words. 'Last night, when I finally persuaded Maria to confess the truth to her family, there was much anger and sorrow, as you can suppose. But Stavros has agreed to the marriage, and Maria and one of her brothers went to the hut and brought him down to face his obligations.' His mouth twisted. 'He was a sight to be pitied.'

'Please don't ask me to try,' she said. 'And now will you please get out of my room? I'm waiting to get dressed.'

The dark eyes watched her. 'Last night you were naked in my arms,' he said. 'So, why this sudden desire for modesty?'

'Because that was last night.' Gemma stared at the floor. 'And this is today, and everything has changed.'

'Why, yes *agape mou*,' he drawled. 'For one thing, I have asked you to marry me.'

'And I have refused.' Gemma lifted her chin defiantly.

'May I know why?'

'I should have thought that was fairly obvious. If Mike hadn't turned up like this, you wouldn't have asked me. Yesterday, all you could think of was getting me off the island. Well, I prefer to stick to the original plan.'

'You don't understand at all,' he said with exasperation. '*Matia mou*, I felt I had to send you away, for your own sake, so that no word of this would ever leak out to involve us in scandal.'

'You mean, you didn't want your own involvement known,' she accused angrily. 'Everyone at the hotel yesterday was staring at me, wondering where you'd picked me up. I suppose I must be a disappointment after your usual ladies.'

'That is nonsense.' He was angry now.

'Is it?' Gemma pushed her hair back wearily. 'Not that it matters. So, please don't feel guilty on my account. As we've established already, it wasn't rape, and I—wanted everything that happened last night, so please don't worry about me—about anything, in fact.'

'What are you saying?' He sounded incredulous. 'That we should pretend all this never happened— that we never met, perhaps?' He walked over to her, cupping her unwilling face between his hands, staring down at her. 'Gemma *mou*, you know that is impossible. Too much has happened. We can never be free of each other, even if that is what we wanted—which I do not believe,' he added flatly. 'So, why will you not marry me?'

'For all kinds of reasons.' The gentleness of his hands against her soft skin made her want to weep, but she controlled the impulse rigidly. 'Because I have a life of my own—a career back in England, and—and I don't need you.'

'And what of my needs?' The smile curving his lips and gleaming in his eyes was a seduction in itself.

Gemma looked away hastily. 'I'm sure Fraulein Gretz will be only too happy to take care of them,' she said tonelessly.

He made a sound that was suspiciously like a choked back laugh. 'Perhaps she would, *agape mou*, if I gave her the opportunity, which I promise you I do not intend to do.'

'Not even at the cosy dinner you were suggesting next week?' As soon as the words were out, she regretted them, knowing that she had given him the chance to taunt her with being jealous.

'Not at any time. Gemma *mou*, I may not have lived like a saint, but I do not seduce women guests in my hotels. Besides, at this cosy dinner you speak of, I had planned to announce our marriage.'

'Is that why you suddenly want a wife?' she asked huskily. 'As protection against predatory blondes?'

He groaned. 'No, wildcat, it is not.' His eyes flicked restlessly past her to the bed, and his mouth curled wryly. 'Damn your brother. If he was not here, I would take you to bed and make love to you until you pleaded with me to marry you.'

'Then I can only be thankful he is here,' she said inimically. 'And you should be grateful, too, because marriage between us would be a disaster. We're strangers from two different worlds, who've just happened to—collide for a brief while, that's all.' She paused, struggling to control the faint quiver in her voice. 'Now, please leave me alone,' she added with desperation.

He gave her a hard, searching look, and she had to force herself to stand her ground and look back at him, as if she meant every word, as if she didn't care.

Then suddenly, starkly, he let her go, and she watched him cross the room, and go out, closing the door behind him.

She said under her breath, 'Oh God,' then her legs gave way, and she sank down, trembling, on to the floor, and stayed there, her arms wrapped round her body, rocking slightly like an unhappy child, while scalding tears emptied down her face.

*   *   *

A shower helped, later, and the tan-and-white dress, which was crisp and pretty, gave her courage too.

But when she got downstairs, only Mike was there, sitting on the terrace drinking coffee. 'He's gone down to the village to make sure the wedding truce is still holding up,' he said, passing her a cup of coffee. 'He's a dynamic bastard when he gets going, I'll say that for him,' he added with grudging admiration. 'I can't altogether blame you for having a little fling with him, Gem, no matter what the original reason. I shouldn't think he often has to ask twice, if ever.'

She said levelly, 'I suppose not.' She paused. 'Mike, can you drive the jeep?'

'Probably,' he said. 'Why?'

'I need to get to Heraklion to catch this plane.'

'Isn't Nikolaides driving you there?' He sounded surprised. 'He mentioned something about it.'

'Perhaps so,' she said. 'But I'd rather it was you, Mike. I don't really want to be alone with him again.'

'You can't get up to much in a jeep,' he said. 'But I'll mention it to him, certainly. I can't see why he should object. Under the circumstances he must be as keen to be rid of you, as you are to leave.' He frowned a little. 'I was hoping I'd be able to stay here again, but if he's in residence, I shall have to look elsewhere. Maybe someone in the village will put me up.'

'I'm sure they will,' she said drily. 'They'll probably be anxious to "make amends" too. But I don't think Andreas will be staying on here. He has an apartment in his hotel at Aghios Nikolaos. I expect he'll be returning there.'

He brightened. 'You think so? Well, here's

hoping. I like this place.' He yawned. 'I don't know about you, but I'm starving. I think I'll go down to the bakery and get some bread.'

'Maria usually brings it.'

'I expect Maria has other things on her mind today,' he said cheerfully, demonstrating, his sister thought wryly, yet again his unparalleled capacity for detachment. He went off whistling.

Gemma finished her coffee, then went upstairs to finish her packing. She put the lace tablecloth in on top of everything else and closed the case. She wanted to leave now, although it was far too early for her plane. She would rather drag round Heraklion, toting her case, than stay at the villa, listening to the moments pass, waiting for the time when she would never see Andreas again, she told herself wretchedly.

When she went downstairs, they had both returned, Mike with bread, and Andreas with a bundle wrapped in paper, which he handed to her.

'What is it?' She made a poor attempt at a smile. 'Another present from a wellwisher?'

He said coldly and briefly, 'Your bag. You could hardly leave without it.'

She bit her lip. 'Well, now I do have it, I'd like to leave right away please.'

He shrugged. 'If it is convenient for your brother, then I have no objections. Besides, I have other plans for the rest of the day,' he added softly.

In spite of what he had said earlier, she had an image of Helga displaying her golden body beside the pool, and winced inwardly.

Mike carried her case out and stowed it in the jeep, grumbling cheerfully at the weight of it.

Gemma faced Andreas. She felt helpless, totally

lost for words, and the dark cool face gave her no help whatsoever.

In the end, she managed a torn 'Goodbye,' then turned and hurried down the terrace steps and through the garden to where the jeep was waiting outside the gate. Mike was already in the driving seat, but as she took her place beside him, he uttered an impatient exclamation.

'I've left my wallet in the rucksack. Hang on, Gem. I won't be long.'

She hoped with all her heart that he wouldn't be. The pain was beginning already, cramping her throat, making breathing difficult. She put her folded arms on the dashboard, and rested her forehead on them, closing her eyes wearily.

Life went on, she told herself, and no one had ever died of a broken heart, or any similar self-inflicted wound.

But it would be easier once she was on her way.

She was aware of his return, aware of the jeep starting up, and she sat up slowly, pushing her tumbled hair back from her face as the vehicle began to lurch down the rough track towards the village.

She froze, her lips parting in a soundless gasp. She said, 'You! But Mike was driving me.'

'A last minute change of plan.'

'Like hell there is.' She wrenched at the door handle, almost breaking a nail. 'Let me out of here.' And as the jeep gathered speed. 'I said—let me out.'

'I heard you,' he hurled back at her. 'I should imagine the whole village heard you also. Now, be quiet.'

'I won't be quiet.' Her voice shook. 'Where is Mike? What have you done with him?'

'He is finishing his breakfast,' he said coolly.

'We talked on our way back from the village, he and I, and arrived at an understanding.'

'How nice for you,' she said wildly. 'Now, stop this bloody jeep. I am not going to Heraklion with you.'

'No, you are not,' he agreed. 'That is another change of plan. We are going to Rethymnon instead.'

She said dangerously, 'And why should we do any such thing?'

'Because my mother has a house there, and I am taking you to stay with her.'

The news struck her dumb, but not for long. 'You'll do no such thing,' she raged at him. 'I don't want to meet your mother, and I'm damned sure she won't have the slightest desire to meet me.'

'Don't be a fool.' He clashed the gears and swore. 'Every mother wishes to meet the girl her son intends to marry.'

'For the last time.' Gemma's voice rose. 'I am not going to marry you.'

She saw him grin. 'I am glad you say that for the last time, *agape mou*. I confess I would prefer you to take a more positive view of our relationship, because you, my wild dove, are going to be my wife just as soon as it can be arranged.'

Tears threatened perilously. She said in a low voice, 'You can't marry me, and you know it. We—we're totally different.'

He shot her a smiling glance. 'Why, yes. You are a woman, and I am a man. That seems to be the usual arrangement.'

'Don't make jokes.' She shook her head helplessly. 'I'm trying to be serious.'

'Marriage is a serious business,' he agreed

solemnly. 'That is why I have avoided it until now.'

'But I'm not from your world,' she said desperately. 'Don't you see how impossible it is?'

He swung the jeep across the road, and brought it to a halt, just under the signpost where James and Hilary had deposited her an eternity before.

He turned to her, and he wasn't smiling any more. Under the smooth olive skin, his face looked taut and drawn.

He said, 'Without you, Gemma *mou*, I have no world. Don't you know that? I love you, and I am so afraid that if I let you go back to England, even for a few days, that I will lose you somehow. That when I follow, you will have escaped me at last, hidden somewhere, and I won't know how to find you.' He touched her cheek with his hand, and she realised he was trembling. 'Stay with me here, treasure of my life and let me teach you to love me. Let me make up to you for all the bitterness that has been between us.'

In a little shaken voice, she said, 'You say—you love me? But how can you? You don't know me.'

'What do I not know?' he asked. 'I know that you love your family, and that you have loyalty and integrity, and fierce courage. I know that you have a temper, and a sense of humour. I know that when we make love, you give yourself with your whole heart, even though you are still too shy to look at me afterwards. Whatever else there is, it will be my joy to learn as we live together.'

She made a little stifled sound. 'You're—very kind.' She didn't look at him. 'But you don't have to say these things. I know you only offered to marry me—to make amends—and because you think you may have made me pregnant.'

He said very gently, 'My sweet one, that is not

true. From the moment I saw you, looking at the Lily-Prince, I wanted you—before even I heard your friend speak your name, and knew for certain who you were.' He groaned. 'And when I realised that you were the girl I was seeking—I felt sick to my stomach. I hated Stavros and his claims on my friendship—hated myself—the whole mess which would stop me meeting you, and wooing you as I wished to do.' His voice deepened huskily. 'That first evening, when I asked you to pretend with me that we were simply lovers, with no complications except our need for each other, I meant every word, *agape mou*. Because, but for Maria and her stupid wicked lies, that is how it would have been for us. Can you deny it?'

'No,' she admitted helplessly. That day at Knossos, she'd already been tinglingly aware of him, although she'd made light of it to Hilary and tried to deny it even to herself, bewildered and disturbed by the strength of her reaction.

'And as for any baby——' His arm went round her shoulders, drawing her to him, and he kissed the corner of her mouth. 'Only God knows if you indeed carry our child under your heart, but I am selfish enough, *matia mou*, to hope that it has not happened yet, so that we will have some time to ourselves to enjoy each other, and to prepare a proper home for the children that will be given to us.' He brushed her mouth with his. 'The apartment at the hotel is unsuitable for a dozen reasons. I want a real home, and you in it. Am I still suffering from egotistical fantasies, my dove?'

She said, 'No,' her mouth trembling into a shy smile as she slid her arms round his neck. 'You make it sound like Paradise, Andreas *mou*.'

He drew her close, and she could feel the urgent,

steady beat of his heart against her breast. *'M'agapas?'* he asked her softly. 'Do you love me?'

'Yes,' she said on a little sigh. 'So much. And I've been so unhappy. I thought you were tired of me, and that was why you were sending me away.'

'Tired of you, wildcat?' His smile teased her. 'I could as soon be tired of life itself. No, I meant to behave so honourably. To send you home, so that I could follow. So that we could start again, with me asking your parents for you—convincing them somehow that I was a suitable husband. Convincing you too if necessary,' he added drily. 'I would have liked to have murdered Maria and Kemal with her, but also I was grateful to them, because the truth set me free to love you as I wanted. And, of course, it then followed that you had to be protected—especially from myself. As my bride to be, your body should have been sacred to me.' He uttered a soft groan. 'But when you came to my room last night, you were a temptation not even a saint could resist, and as I've told you, I've never pretended to be a saint.' His mouth twisted a little. 'So—that is why we go to Rethymnon, to my mother's house, where not even I would dare to be tempted.' He took her hands and raised them to his lips. 'And I think we will not distress either my mother or yours, by giving them any hint that we have already enjoyed our wedding night.'

It was her turn to tease. 'You have an unexpectedly conventional streak, *kyrie*.'

He grinned back at her. 'I intend to be a model husband, *kyria*—your husband.' He stroked her face with his hand. 'So, I ask again, Gemma *mou*, will you marry me. Will you be my life, as I will be yours?'

And she breathed her answer against his lips as she kissed him.

You're invited to accept 4 books and a surprise gift Free!

Acceptance Card

Mail to: Harlequin Reader Service®

In the U.S.
2504 West Southern Ave.
Tempe, AZ 85282

In Canada
P.O. Box 2800, Postal Station A
5170 Yonge Street
Willowdale, Ontario M2N 6J3

YES! Please send me 4 free Harlequin Presents® novels and my free surprise gift. Then send me 8 brand new novels every month as they come off the presses. Bill me at the low price of $1.75 each ($1.95 in Canada) — an 11% saving off the retail price. There are no shipping, handling or other hidden costs. There is no minimum number of books I must purchase. I can always return a shipment and cancel at any time. Even if I never buy another book from Harlequin, the 4 free novels and the surprise gift are mine to keep forever.

108 BPP-BPGE

_____

Name   (PLEASE PRINT)

_____

Address   Apt. No.

_____

City   State/Prov.   Zip/Postal Code

This offer is limited to one order per household and not valid to present subscribers. Price is subject to change.

ACP-SUB-1

EYE OF THE STORM

MAURA SEGER

A powerful portrayal of the events of World War II in the Pacific, *Eye of the Storm* is a riveting story of how love triumphs over hatred. In this, the first of a three-book chronicle, Army nurse Maggie Lawrence meets Marine Sgt. Anthony Gargano. Despite military regulations against fraternization, they resolve to face together whatever lies ahead.... Author Maura Seger, also known to her fans as Laurel Winslow, Sara Jennings, Anne MacNeil and Jenny Bates, was named 1984's Most Versatile Romance Author by *The Romantic Times*.

You're invited to accept 4 books and a surprise gift Free!

Acceptance Card

Mail to: **Harlequin Reader Service**®

In the U.S.
2504 West Southern Ave.
Tempe, AZ 85282

In Canada
P.O. Box 2800, Postal Station A
5170 Yonge Street
Willowdale, Ontario M2N 6J3

YES! Please send me 4 free Harlequin Romance® novels and my free surprise gift. Then send me 6 brand new novels every month as they come off the presses. Bill me at the low price of $1.65 each ($1.75 in Canada)—an 11% saving off the retail price. There are no shipping, handling or other hidden costs. There is no minimum number of books I must purchase. I can always return a shipment and cancel at any time. Even if I never buy another book from Harlequin, the 4 free novels and the surprise gift are mine to keep forever. 116 BPR-BPGE

Name _____ (PLEASE PRINT)

Address _____ Apt. No. _____

City _____ State/Prov. _____ Zip/Postal Code _____

This offer is limited to one order per household and not valid to present subscribers. Price is subject to change. ACR-SUB-1